Deadwood's Deadly Puzzle

Crossword Puzzle Mystery Novella

Louise Foster

Owl Cafe Press LLC

ISBN 978-1-955458-21-4

Eight Letters in Betrayal: A Crossword Puzzle Cozy Mystery

Book Cover by Steven Novak

WHO COMPLAINS ABOUT HAVING TOO MUCH MONEY?

Answer? My latest client.

I'm Tracy Belden, being a PI is one of my three jobs. My client recently acquired a company which is showing an unexpected spike in profits. Worried about illegal activity, she's demanding answers.

So, me, my precocious, crime solving twelve-year-old son, and my family are headed to Deadwood, South Dakota. However,the possibility of fraud turns to tragedy when I find one of the former partners poisoned.

Was his death suicide or murder? Either way, to complete my puzzle, I have to find the secret his death was meant to hide.

Contents

1

14 Across; 8 Letters;
Clue: Antagonistic manner.
Answer: Attitude.

"I don't like you." Pam Isley, co-owner of a major corporation in Nevada, didn't bother to disguise her disdain.

If I were kind, I might put her rude comment down to the fact that she was fighting a takeover bid by her disinherited deadbeat sister. However, that wasn't the cause of her imperious attitude. She'd been born that way.

What amazed me was that Pam or anyone else believed that I, Tracy Rae Belden, P.I., cared what they thought of me. Outside of my family or friends, the world could go whistle in the wind and I wouldn't lose a minute of sleep.

"Yeah, that's great. I'm crushed."I managed to swallow the long-suffering sigh that rose up. No way could I keep the boredom out of my voice.

What did she expect me to say? "I don't like you either", came to mind. However, as of this morning, she was a paying client of Crawford Investigations, owned by my boss Crawford.

Thankfully, Pam's company was headquartered in Lake Tahoe. I lived in Langsdale, Nevada, a three-hour drive north of Vegas.

"What you did to the Prushark family was unforgivable." The woman continued in a strident tone. "Your investigation crushed them. I grew up with their children."

"Hey! Don't kill the messenger."The words broke through what little restraint I had. "I didn't kill old man Prushark. All I did was prove who murdered him."

I was losing patience with her attitude. I'd been in a good mood before this phone call. Glancing at the crossword puzzle I'd been working on creating, I pushed away the laptop. That would also prevent me from being distracted by looking at the spreadsheet of B&T, Inc.

My ten-year bestie, Kevin Tanner and I had joined forces in the handyman company a few months ago. Only weeks ago, we'd joined in marriage.

Determined to focus on my P.I. job,I told myself to act like an adult. In an effort to recoup the situation, I stifled another sigh and decided to focus on the case. "Let's move past the pleasantries. What's the case? Crawford didn't provide me with any details."

Actually, the froggy voiced rat had told me next to nothing.

"Pam Isley has a job." He'd growled when he called. "She paid up front and insisted on you. She'll call you. Keep quiet and get results."

What was I supposed to do with that lead in? Play nice with a woman who disliked me?

"I asked for you because you come up with results." Pam spoke in a tight, autocratic tone. "How you manage to succeed, I'll never know. However, I have little to lose by throwing you at the problem."

"Isn't that sweet?" My impatient hind brain took control when I wasn't looking. Was it good or bad that the words dripped with a syrupy, patently fake tone? "What is the high stakes issue I'm going to spend my time on?"

Stony silence met my comeback. Her long, drawn-out exhale signaled her rising temper. "You are *so* annoying."

"It's what I do." I shot back. "Go with my strength."

"One of the companies I recently acquired is having issues." Pam's voice reverted to a professional tone.

My brain clicked over to business as well. We'd both be better off sticking to the facts. "What kind of issues?Personal? Financial?"

"Both." Came the terse reply.

That was going to be my third guess. "How long have you owned the company?"

"Almost three months." She answered immediately. "The ninety-day probationary period is coming up next week. Our people audited the books before and after the sale. Everything balances, but the numbers aren't what they should be based on the market and the supplies. The area doesn't... shouldn't have the base to justify the recent sales."

Her words brought me up short."Wait a minute. Your new business is bringing in too *much* money?"

My brain grabbed hold of the dichotomy with both hands. I had to give the other woman points for originality. Very few clients complain of an excess of profits. However, while touchy, feely emotions aren't my strength, numbers are, and in any equation both sides have to balance.

"I realize this isn't a common problem." Pam clipped off her words with a knife's edge. A hard anger colored her tone.

Her ire flowed over me without effect as the puzzle caught my attention. "How many audits have been done?"

A small huff sounded over the line.

"A full audit before the purchase,of course." When she spoke this time, her voice was much calmer. "No problems were flagged. Three weeks after the sale the first reports came in. We'd put money into renovations. However, I never expected this rapid of a turnaround. The VP in charge and I agreed a second audit was needed."

I focused on her update. "The second audit balanced also?"

I knew the answer. If the numbers hadn't balanced, Pam would have dug into the discrepancy on her own. She wouldn't have hired Crawford, and she wouldn't be on the phone with me.

"The sales and profits matched to the last dollar." Her strident tone betrayed her worry. For the first time in the conversation, I felt a kinship with the woman. "I *know* something is off, but I have no proof."

It was the gut, as Marcus, my precocious twelve-year-old son often said about me. If an answer didn't silence my internal worries, I kept looking until I was satisfied.

A deep felt exhale echoed over the line. "I bought the business on the advice of a longtime employee. Warren Kitt was born in South Dakota. He's worked for me for twenty years. The business was under performing. It's a minor company in my portfolio, but I don't appreciate being made a fool of."

"Did you have someone local investigate?" I asked. "Or do you think they'll be too close to the issue?"

"I don't want anyone who might be compromised." Her stern tone brooked no argument. "For all your rumored faults-"

Gee, thanks. I rolled my eyes at her jab.

"All my reports agree that you can't be bought." Pam sounded disappointed. "Honestly, it sounds like you don't listen to anyone. I don't understand why Crawford tolerates you."

"Because I solve puzzles," I retorted. "And I get results."

"Fine. I want answers." Her tone turned professional. "I'll forward you the information I have. You leave tomorrow."

"Tomorrow?" No one mentioned such a quick deadline. "You might not think so, but I have a life. A husband. A child.A business of my own."

Pam scoffed. "I'm certain they can live without you for a few days. This is important."

I gritted my teeth as our fellowship evaporated. "I'll make arrangements with Crawford regarding when I can leave."

In a remarkable show of restraint,I hung up before I said something Crawford would regret. I stuck my tongue out at the phone. My brain calculated the cost of insisting on a first-class plane ticket against turning it in for five cheap seats.

There was no way I'd be able to leave town on a case for Crawford without taking my twelve-year-old Sherlock Holmes wannabe along. Then, there was the rest of the Belden-Tanner Detective Agency as my son Marcus had dubbed our adopted family.

And where would Holmes be without his seventy-plus Dr. Watson? Mrs. C, my landlady and friend, was even British.

I tapped the phone against my chin.A surplus of money was a difficult oddity to explain. At least, this case had no dead bodies.

2

11 Down; 5 Letters;
Clue: A ploy or scheme.
Answer: Trick.

Marcus, my twelve-year-old adopted son, grimaced at me from the other side of the gray sectional in our loft apartment. His dusky skin and straight black hair were clear evidence of his Korean heritage. "Couldn't you find a crime in San Diego? Or Orlando?"

"I'm sure I *could* find a crime there," I said, staring right back at him. I'd taken the boy child off the streets four years ago after he stole my wallet, and ran away with my heart. "But no one's paying me to fly to a coast and solve those fictitious crimes. Pam Isley *is* paying me to investigate what's happening at her newly acquired business in Deadwood, South Dakota."

Mrs. Alice Colchester, otherwise known as Mrs. C, set a second large bowl of buttery popcorn on the coffee table. "I've never been to Deadwood. This could be a bit of a lark."

Kevin Tanner, my hubby of only a few weeks, filled a smaller bowl with popcorn and passed the large one to Jack Rabi. "South Dakota's new territory for me, too. We can check out old western towns, Mount Rushmore, the Badlands."

I nudged his shoulder. "That's the spirit!"

Marcus's expression morphed into one of excitement. "The Badlands! That sounds right up our alley. They must have gunfights set up in some of those towns, too."

Rabi, a black man with ashen skin and shoulder length black hair that fell in waves to his shoulders, put the large bowl of popcorn between him and Marcus. "Got the week off."

That was a display of wild enthusiasm for him. A former member of Special Ops for twenty-two years, he'd been adopted as family within a week of Marcus moving in with me. The lean man was slightly over six-feet tall but his frame had slightly more meat on it than a cadaver.

"Good!" I cuddled up next to Kevin. "Let's start the movie. What are we watching by the way?"

""The Sting" with Newman and Redford." Marcus aimed the remote at the television. "Rabi and I chose it for Kevin."

Which meant Marcus picked the movie. I frowned at the boy's supposed motive. "Do you think this movie can teach Kevin anything about grifting?"

My hubby had been born and raised in the internationally famous Feilen family of con artists. At six-foot-one with black hair and eyes the color of sapphires, his charm and brains had landed the family millions of dollars in scams. Unfortunately for them, he'd been born with a conscience. Ten years ago, he walked away from it all for the glamorous life of a construction worker and living paycheck to paycheck.

Kevin chuckled at my question. There was nothing he didn't know about running scams.

Marcus waved away my comment. "This movie is a kinder, gentler view of grifting. Besides, I like it."

Kevin put a hand on my leg. "What business did Pam Isley invest in, and why did she choose South Dakota?"

Having spent the last couple of hours reading over the material Pam sent me and doing my own research, I had an answer at hand. "Pam has some interests in that area. She also took advantage of several tax incentives for investments in agribusiness research and tourism. Her new business researches the use of solar panels on farms and ranches to benefit crops and livestock. The company also sells rare and specialty wines, and they have a micro-brewery."

"That's an odd range of interests." Kevin eyed me as he munched popcorn. "Tax dodge?"

"I think so." My head hurt from trying to decipher the various holdings of the company they'd bought out. "One of Pam's trusted managers, Warren Kitt works remotely from South Dakota. He proposed the takeover after doing the initial prospectus."

Mrs. C looked up from her knitting project. Under her perfectly coiffed white curls, her green eyes narrowed. "Green energy is the latest golden child, innit? Solar panels should be bang on for a company."

"You'd think, wouldn't you?" I was still getting a handle on the case. "The solar panel division was on top of the latest research. Development was getting off the ground. They had some sales, but their grants ran out. Loans were coming due and they'd failed to show a profit after four years."

"Ripe for a buyout." My hubby looked absorbed in Paul Newman's struggle to get a carousel running in the movie.

Grifters knew how businesses worked. Kevin had faked being an executive or an investor numerous times in his short life as a con artist.

"You nailed it." I confirmed his supposition, not surprised he'd guessed correctly. "A young couple and three friends got together in college. None of them could make a go of it by themselves. They pooled their business acumen and their money."

Marcus, munching popcorn, split his wide-eyed interest evenly between Newman and my report. "This is where it gets good. Money. Envy. Hurt feelings. Anger. I like it."

I wanted to tell him to concentrate on the movie. However, having survived the streets on his own for a few years, he'd seen the seamier side of life. Besides, the decision to sell was the most likely spot to plant seeds of discourse.

I tipped my head to the boy child. "Two of the guys signed non-competitive forms regarding the solar panel division and took a buyout. One is working in Deadwood."

Kevin seemingly watched the movie with undivided interest. Until his eyes narrowed. "He oversaw the winery and the brews?"

At my nod, Marcus slapped the sofa. "How did you know?"

The boy had taken the words right out of my mouth.

Kevin didn't take his gaze from the television screen. "If he was interested in the solar panel development, he'd have stayed rather than walk away. A high-end restaurant or shop that deals in fine wines would give him leave to dabble without competing."

"Score one for Tanner." I thought back to my notes. "The other buyout returned home to North Carolina. He's working at his family's boating business on the coast."

"That leaves three." Marcus held up three fingers. "Are the married couple the brains? What about the third person?"

This was the crux of the issue as I saw it. "The married couple, Natalie and Matt Crocker, along with Yvonne Dunston stayed with the company. They were given titles as VP's of Research and Development. The other staff were left intact. A handful of Isley employees were shifted to oversee the whole. Development was set to continue uninterrupted."

Mrs. C, who'd added jalapeno salt to her popcorn, followed my report with interest. "When did the problem first develop?"

I met the older woman's gaze without glancing at my notes. "A month after the sale, the wineries and micro-brews showed a marked rise in sales. It's seen steady growth ever since."

"Wait a minute!" Marcus yelled and threw up his hands. "What was all that about the solar panels and research, lady?"

Seeing equally puzzled expressions on the others, I held up my hands to forestall the protests. "The original five partners figured diversity would give them a greater chance of success. Atherton, the guy in town, inherited a huge wine cellar and wanted to build on that. The other buyout, Hayden had a micro-brewery business. They bought a small company dealing with solar panels, which was supposed to bring in the big bucks."

The explanation mollified some of the outrage.

I continued painting the picture. "They share the profits from any part of the venture."

Kevin watched me closely. "Deadwood is built on tourism. The wine sale and microbrewery should have been a shoe in. What went wrong?"

"That's the question." I'd been studying the issue and the people all day. "Natalie Crocker is skilled in getting grants and loans, but the solar panel division ate money from the beginning. They poured cash into research and production. The wine and beer sales kept them afloat, but not enough. Once the sale went though, the wine and beer sales shot up."

Marcus abandoned Newman and Redford. He leaned his elbows on his knees and faced me with a scrunched-up expression. "You were hired because the company's making money? Who does that?"

I threw my notes on the coffee table that sat in the middle of the sectional. "That is the one thing Pam and I see eye-to-eye on. Having those sections of the company turn a profit *now* doesn't make sense."

"If the original partners were so close to making good, why sell?" Kevin's face wore a thoughtful expression. "They had to know how the numbers were running."

A low, ruminating hum sounded from Mrs. C. "The men in charge of the two divisions turning a profit took the money and walked away? That's rather odd."

"Exactly!" My mind had been stacking the information all day, probing for holes or threads to pull. "I don't have any answers in my puzzle."

"This trip should be great." My son grabbed a handful of popcorn. "We're going to Deadwood, except nobody's dead."

With his laughter echoing around the room at his feeble joke, I shook my head and turned to the movie.

Pam hadn't warned anyone except her manager, Warren Kitt, that I was coming. If there was fraud, the answer had to lie in the partnership. I doubted the remaining trio would welcome my arrival.

3

24 Across; 6 Letters;
Clue: Opening move.
Answer: Gambit.

I'll skip over the packing and travel. With Marcus fresh out of school and Rabi able to get the week off, we landed in Rapid City, South Dakota two days after I'd spoken with Pam Isley.

Given the exorbitant price of my first-class ticket with only two days warning, turning it in to cover five last minute economy tickets didn't leave too much of a gap. I also flipped what I considered a pricey hotel for a three-bedroom Air B-N-B with a foldout sofa.

I was feeling pretty pleased with myself as we drove down the main street of Deadwood, South Dakota. Small shops and restaurants lined both sides. Colorful awnings mixed with historical names and buildings.

After an early lunch that included chicken fried steak bites at the Nugget Saloon, we settled into our rented house.

Marcus exited the small den after depositing his suitcase on the floor. "Does she really expect you to solve this in, like, five days? Why don't her people look into the problem? Why the hurry?"

"Her people searched for an answer with no luck." I took his rapid-fire questions in stride while glancing at the spacious living area. I was looking forward to mixing my investigation with trips to the Crazy Horse Memorial and Mount Rushmore, along with all the other sights. "The remaining partners are due to receive a final payout this week. She wants answers before that happens, and she's willing to pay extra to get them."

Marcus stopped halfway into the living room. His wide eyes stared out the French Doors at the back of the house. "We have a pool and a hot tub! Hallelujah!"

He threw his arms over his head and stomped in place. "We are rich!"

"We're traveling on someone else's dime." Which was my favorite way to travel. I smiled at my son's antics. "The water does look nice. No reason we can't reconnoiter poolside."

While the rest of us swam, Mrs. C sat under the overhang in a muumuu splashed with bright blooms of every color.

After I'd abandoned the pool for a spot in the sun, Rabi, Marcus and Kevin swam for a while. Finally, they got out and flopped into the remaining chairs, dripping wet.

"Okay," Marcus breathed out the word as he filled a corn chip with an abundance of dip. "Stop stalling. If the Belden-Tanner Agency is going to solve this case, we need all the facts."

I stared at my boy child over the rim of my lemonade. There were several things wrong with his statement. "*I* haven't been playing in the pool for the last half-hour. Besides, I gave you all the facts I have."

We also weren't a detective agency. Only I was an actual PI. The Belden-Tanner Agency was a figment of Marcus's imagination. Although my adopted family had done their part to help me solve several murders, it was strictly voluntary. As in, I didn't share my paycheck. However, they did benefit in other ways. Ala, we were sitting by a pool in Deadwood.

Mrs. C, my seventy-plus landlady, shuffled over in her ever-present slippers. In honor of Deadwood, she'd brought the pair with sheriff badges on them. "What roll are you expected to play? You'll need access to the businesses."

Her British accent was decidedly at odds with the western setting.

Marcus pointed a second chip over-burdened with dip at me. "Are we undercover? We could sneak into places and find their stash."

His dramatic whisper had a sinister tone that was completely at odds with the sunny day and the slight breeze.

"We don't need to sneak in anywhere." I told him in a firm tone. "Only Warren Kitt, Pam's on-site rep knows I've been hired to look into the situation."

Kevin twirled a fork in his fingers. His blue eyes held a discerning gaze. "Does she want you to find answers or does she want to make sure no one else can find the problem? That would explain why she hired someone she considers too stubborn for their own good."

Grabbing a chip for myself, I rewarded my hubby with a smile. "You get the door prize. This investment is a tax dodge. She doesn't want anything illegal, but more than that, she doesn't want trouble."

Marcus snorted back a laugh. "And she hired *you?* Didn't she learn anything from your case with the Prusharks?"

I joined in the round of laughter. "I have a meeting with Warren Kitt in an hour. He's been on-site for several months. He chose the company to purchase. He's followed their profits for a few years. Why he chose them over other contenders, I don't know. An easy sale evidently. He also negotiated and oversaw the sale. As the man in charge, he relocated here."

"He's responsible." Rabi's low drawl cut across the conversation for the first time in several minutes.

"This is his baby." I wondered where Kitt stood on my involvement. "If I find major trouble, he'll have to explain how he missed whatever is going on. I'm not sure he'll welcome me sticking my nose into the game."

Mrs. C unfurled a large fan with orange and yellow flowers on it. She fanned herself with a languid air while eyeing me. "What's your next step?"

Her tone held a skeptical note, knowing my penchant for jumping into cases with no plan at all.

I took a deep breath. I'd considered my options over the last few days. "Pam wants to keep the investigation on the down low. I'll get Warren Kitt's input. See how far he's willing to help or if he has any ideas."

Kevin tapped a rhythm on the table's edge. Water dripped off his black hair. "How did he explain the abnormal jump in profits?"

"He's the one who pointed out the trend to Pam." I was as baffled as everyone else. "He says he's been watching the books, tracing down the new orders, and the businesses they originate from. Everything looks legit."

Mrs. C's pale green eyes narrowed. The older woman had done her share of dancing on the wild side of the law during fifty years of running from a murder charge. A murder, we discovered a few months ago, that she wasn't guilty of. However, she had an excellent understanding of the shady elements of society.

That, coupled with Kevin's grifting background, gave me a wealth of knowledge to draw on. I watched the woman in anticipation.

She leaned back in the chair. "Very odd affair."

My hopes plummeted. I know this is my case, but I'd been hoping for words of wisdom. When I blinked, her Hawaiian themed muumuu, coupled with the puffy sheriff's badge slippers, and the tangerine fan, hit me in the face. What was I thinking?

To be honest, I couldn't blame Mrs. C. I needed more input than Pam saying something was off with this acquisition.

"Here's the plan." I shoved the chips away and dusted off my fingers. My audience eyed me with no visible reactions. "I'm going to meet with Wallace Kitt. You..."

I pointed at them in a slow arc. "Are going to hit the sights of downtown Deadwood."

Marcus perked up. "Like bakeries and ice-cream parlors?"

I eyed the boy child. He, even more than the rest of us, traveled on his stomach "Sure. Check out everything. But you have had three meals already."

He shook his head with a mournful sigh. "Desserts go to a different stomach, T.R. You know that."

Kevin nodded in agreement. "It's true."

"Whatever." I couldn't win when the two of them were in cahoots. "Visit local wine stores and breweries. Does Prairie Sun and Spirits have a good reputation? What's local opinion on Wallace Kitt and the buyout?"

Kevin studied me with a flicker of suspicion in his eyes. "Does something have your goat about this case, Belden?"

I never could hide anything from him. After ten years of being besties, he knew me too well. "I'm wondering if Pam expects me to fail. This set up doesn't make sense, but she knew I couldn't resist a puzzle."

"And you fell into her evil trap." Marcus summed up the affair in a deep, falsely menacing tone.

"I was helpless." I admitted, admitting my inability to turn away from a challenging puzzle.

Kevin's expression softened. His low chuckle morphed into a smile. "We'll scour the town for innuendo and rumor."

Marcus stiffened like a dog on point. "Do these places have like, finger food? Munchies?"

"Seriously?" I eyed our son. "Is that all you think of?"

"I'm a growing boy." His straight, black hair, drying in the hot sun, flew around his face as he threw back his head. "You can write it off on the expense report, and we'll get the information you need. People love us."

He pasted on a charming expression.

I sighed. It was true. Heaven help the denizens of Deadwood. "I'm glad I have a meeting to go to. Please don't call me with any catastrophes."

4

42 Down; 6 Letters;

Clue: Critical situation; ______ play.

Answer: Clutch.

Warren Kitt's office was as nondescript as the man himself. He was two inches shorter than my five-nine height. He made no pretense of hiding either his thinning hair or his growing belly. At forty-four, he was almost a decade older than me. Though he had a laid back manner, the hazel eyes behind his eye-glasses held a sharp intelligence.

Housed in an unassuming building several blocks away from the small, but thriving downtown area, the front man for the Isley Corporation led me into a twelve-by-fifteen-foot room. Ignoring the oak desk opposite the door, he led me to a polished oval table containing several folders and a laptop.

"Please, have a seat, Ms. Belden." He waved me to a chair facing the door before sitting next to me. "The files regarding the Prairie Sun and Spirits Company are at your disposal. Pam asked me to give you any help I can. I only hope you're able to get to the bottom of this manner. Where would you like to start?"

I couldn't stop the groan that escaped at the sight of the reports or the offer to go through the figures again. Raising my gaze from the death traps, my eyes locked in on the espresso machine on a counter behind the door.

My entire body froze. Putting a hand over my heart, I let myself get lost in the moment. Next to my family, coffee is my first love. I pointed at the gleaming silver. "Does that make coffee? And call me Tracy."

A smile wreathed his face reminiscent of a proud papa. "Call me Warren, and that makes the best coffee in the entire state. I recently received a bag of orange Amaretto coffee beans. Would you like a cup?"

I couldn't even speak. All I could do was nod and hope Warren wasn't guilty of any wrong doing, because he was my new best friend. Kevin would understand.

Moments later, I inhaled the delicious aroma of the freshly brewed cup. The scent alone was enough to breathe new life into my veins. Taking a sip, I let the hot brew settle on my tongue. "Ooohh! This is ambrosia."

"Wait!" Warren's satisfied expression grew even more excited. "I have fresh baked Ginger Snap cookies from the local bakery. You have to try them with this coffee. They're to die for."

"Oh, my!" With a bite of the cookie still on my tongue, I took another sip of coffee and let the flavors mingle. "This is delicious. I may never leave."

Warren chuckled. Then, his mouth flattened. "Not if you're looking for answers."

"And reality rears its ugly head." I set down my cup and turned my attention to the case. "I know numbers, but I'm no expert. If you can't find fault with the figures, I doubt I will. For the moment, let's say you're not behind the issue I've been hired to investigate."

Crawford's people were actually going over the books right now. I'd learned not to show all my cards in an investigation.

"Thank you for your trust." He spoke in a heartfelt tone.

"It's not that." I couldn't afford to trust anyone on a case, not even people who served me heavenly tasting coffee and cookies. "You pointed out the... let's call making too much money a problem for the moment."

Warren gave me a rueful smile and toasted me with his I Love Deadwood coffee cup.

I continued. "Also, if your goal was to commit fraud, there are more options in company headquarters in Tahoe."

"Along with greater scrutiny." Warren pointed out in a show of honesty.

"Why did you ask to oversee a company in Deadwood at this point in your career?" I asked. A quick check had showed he hadn't been born or gone to school in South Dakota. "Your social media shows pictures of a Mason family reunion in Mitchell, South Dakota."

"You *are* thorough." Surprise and admiration showed in his eyes. "My family settled here four generations ago. My sister and brother moved to the state in the last five years. One for a job. The other to help with the family store in Mitchell, South Dakota. When I read about the Prairie Sun and Spirits' diverse interests and their failing cash flow, the company seemed like the investment opportunity-"

"Tax dodge." I inserted with a smile.

Warren chuckled. "The Isley Corporation has been looking for smaller companies to invest in. If it goes well, I'll transfer here full-time. I have nothing keeping me in Nevada."

His unblinking gaze and manner lent him an air of honesty, but I don't get paid to take people at their word. "Would you mind giving me your siblings names and addresses?"

With an expectant look on his face, he took a piece of paper out of a folder and slid it toward me.

"Due diligence." I explained, glancing at the names before sliding the paper into my purse. "Currently, I'm stuck on the motive. I can't figure out an end-game. The profit ends up in the Isley account. Nobody launders money without wanting the cash back somehow. I assume the profits are safe?"

"Absolutely. The money is in our accounts." Warren adjusted his accountant-like glasses. A slight tightening of his eyes increased his wrinkles. His glance strayed to the files and reports on the table.

I noted his reaction while cringing at the thought of more reading. I also believed the answer lay in the ties that had bound the original partners together. "Tell me about Natalie and Matt Crocker. The married couple that put their dreams into spreading solar panels across the open fields of South Dakota."

Warren's eyes relaxed along with his shoulders as we shifted topics. Most of what he told me, I already knew. Natalie could have made a living as a grant writer. Matt was the front man and a whiz at sales. Yvonne Dunston was a computer expert. She'd created the computer programs they still used after the buyout. He hadn't had much contact with Bruce Atherton, the wine guy in town, and had never met Tom Hayden, living on a boat off the east coast.

Warren couldn't point to any red flags, but my brain was busily arranging clues and a grid for my mental crossword puzzle. After conning him out of a cup of coffee for the road, Warren stopped me at the door.

"Tracy, this venture was my idea." He met my gaze with a desperate air. "I want to stay here permanently. I've grown to love this area and being close to my family. If there's anything I can do, let me know. I'll throw in a bag of the orange Amaretto and Ginger Snap cookies if you find the answer."

"You know how to hit me where I live." If I'd needed incentive to solve this puzzle, I had it. Perhaps I should get the promise in writing in case he was guilty. "I'll keep in touch."

"Great. You can copy me on the reports you send Pam."

I shook his hand, throwing in a smile at his assumption. I didn't mention that my boss would be lucky to get a report. I had no intention of communicating with Pam Isley.

Several moments later I connected with the rest of the Belden-Tanner Agency at a small park by the Halloway Rodeo Cowboy statue. They were eating ice cream from the Big Dipper. I ditched my empty cup of amaretto coffee. Planting a kiss on Kevin's cheek, I settled myself into a wooden picnic table. Situated under a row of trees, the place provided a perfect spot for people watching.

Marcus's eagle eyes nailed me with a stern stare. "What have you learned? Do you know who did it?"

In the act of stealing a drink from Kevin's smoothie, I made the boy wait before gifting him with a frown. "I've been in town for a few hours. I'm gathering information. What about-"

"Good." The boy breathed a sigh. "There are cowboy reenactments and we need to go on the stagecoach ride. We have to stay long enough to do everything."

"I'm glad you have your priorities in order." I gave the boy a flat stare. "As long we're making lists, no one can go on the tour of Victorian houses without me."

Mrs. C, looking comfortable with her muumuu, waved her fan at me. "I can't wait to see the Victorians. I'm with you."

Marcus's initial grimace deepened. He looked wildly back and forth from Kevin to Rabi as he made a slashing motion across his throat.

Kevin chuckled. "I'll be happy to escort you both. Rabi and Marcus can find something else to do. Maybe find the barns where they keep the horses."

"That would be cool!" Marcus jumped at the alternative. Then, like a camera shutter, his manner shifted. He looked around our mostly deserted corner of the park before leaning forward. "What have you learned? You go first. Then, we'll tell you what we heard."

With his tantalizing promise hanging in the air, I gave an abbreviated version of Warren's updates. "Hayden has made brief visits, but Kitt's never met the guy in person. Atherton jumped at the buyout because he was unhappy with the partnership, possibly from the beginning. The venture was built on his business acumen and a wine cellar of rare vintages he inherited that partially funded the early years."

"An outlier." Narrowed eyes accompanied Rabi's judgement.

I was struck with the accuracy of his guess. "The five of them came together in during college. The last three partners have always been a united front."

Mrs. C's sly smile and knowing green eyes met me when I looked up. "More than you know, luv."

Her British accent and intriguing comment put me in mind of an Agatha Christie scene at a country house.

The boy child, having scanned the table for buy-in, leaned forward. "Yvonne dated Matt in college. He joined the scheme with Bruce, who introduced the two them. Tell her, Kevin."

My hubby, having waited his turn, nodded solemnly at being given the stage. "Matt and Yvonne dated for several weeks. Natalie and Hayden had been soulmates for two years. She was the driving force behind the business, but she needed money."

Mrs. C snapped her multi-colored fan together. Her eyes twinkled at the whiff of intrigue. "Matt inherited a trust fund months later when he turned twenty-one. That's what Natalie wanted, and she got it, didn't she?"

"She dumped Hayden for Matt Crocker? And the partnership survived?" I couldn't imagine why Yvonne or Hayden had stayed. I said as much. "Perhaps they were banking on the profits coming in after the lean times."

"Too much lean time." Rabi's mouth barely moved as he delivered the summation. His gaze continued to scan the area.

I sipped the dregs of Kevin's smoothie, flashing him a smile. "The team invested heavily in the solar panels anticipating sales and a grant that didn't materialize. The loss of capital sapped the bottom line."

Mrs. C clicked her tongue. "And the dominoes fell into the Isley's lap, didn't they?"

Marcus cupped his chin in his hands. "Can't the increased sales just be, like, a cycle or something?"

I nodded at the insight behind his observation. It wasn't a bad question. "On the surface, that's a possibility. But when Warren considered what's selling, the numbers don't make sense."

"Why not?" Marcus held out a hand as he spoke. "And, you still can't solve the case before the end of the week."

"I don't think that's going to be a problem." Since I had no clue what was going on. "The increased profits aren't tied only to the sale of the wine and beers. The sale of merchandise like t-shirts, hats, and cups is topping out. The rate is out-performing more established wineries and breweries. The purchases are legitimate as near as the accountants can tell."

Interest sparked in Kevin's eyes. His fingers beat a rhythm on his glass. I waited but he said nothing.

"You have an idea?" I prompted. I was out of my depth. I'd never had any excess money to worry about.

He met my gaze before shifting to Mrs. C. "Have you ever laundered money?"

The older woman pursed her lips. "I've had the odd occasion to shift money, shall we say, luv."

Marcus's eyebrows rose. "Your family probably moved money lots of times, huh Kevin?"

"On occasion," Kevin parroted with a smile accompanied by a thoughtful look. Finally, he shook his head. "This doesn't follow any pattern I've seen. This company isn't on the stock market."

"Nope." I shook my head. "Privately owned from the beginning, still is under Isley. The money is rolling in for Isley and no one knows why. How would you like to discuss rare wines with Bruce Atherton? I made an appointment with him in your name. We could eat at the Legends Steakhouse."

Kevin narrowed his gaze at the teasing note in my voice. "A walk in the park and a fancy eatery, all in one day? I could be convinced."

A loud slap on the table made me jump.

"No!" Marcus wailed. "There's a shootout tonight. We have to go. Rabi, you'd rather go see cowboys, right?"

"Every time." The man sounded insulted at even being asked.

"Mrs. C?" the boy pointed at the older woman. "You're in, too?"

"Wouldn't miss it for the world." The woman's face was wreathed in a smile of anticipation. "I do love a good shootout!"

If it were any other soul over seventy, I'd take the comment for a joke. With Mrs. C, it was probably the truth.

"Oh, no!" Kevin slumped in his seat. His face was a mask of anguish.

Concern coursed through me. "What's wrong?"

My hubby groaned. He leaned toward Marcus. "I have to go to dinner alone with Belden?"

I glared at Kevin while trying to keep a straight face.

Marcus roared with laughter and pointed at Kevin. "You like her, Kev. That's why you married her. You have to take her."

I playfully pushed my hubby away as he reached for me. "For that, you're buying me dessert, and you aren't getting an invitation to the pizza party when we solve the case."

Kevin laughed in the face of my threat, kissing my cheek.

Marcus waved his hand. "You can be my plus one, Kev."

"You're lucky you have him." I grinned at my husband and best friend. "Now, take me home so I can get dolled up for this dinner. I intend to ambush Bruce Atherton, and you're going to help."

"Let's go!" Kevin leapt to his feet. "I better be looking good for this, too."

As if the man could look bad.

***

Fast forward to late afternoon, Rabi, Mrs. C, and Marcus were last seen headed for the shootout. Kevin and I had strolled hand-in-hand down Main Street. We meandered through two art galleries and strolled through multiple tourist shops with their colorful awnings. I'd noted the sign for Big Dipper offering ice cream, then spent several minutes admiring the stunning jewels in the Ponderosa Trading Company. Finally, we at a delicious meal ate Legends with their matchless service.

Kevin squeezed my hand. "The Buffalo Wine Barrel's up ahead. I reviewed their wines in stock. It's good stuff."

I hugged his arm and kissed his cheek. "That's why I keep you."

"Had to be something," he said with a teasing smile. "How do you want to handle this? Subtle? Or your way?"

"I'm not in the mood for subtle."

"Are you *ever*?"

"My gut thinks the problem lies with the odd combination of people." I admitted. "That back story doesn't add up for me, and Miss Marple told me not to believe what people say."

"Miss Marple should know." Despite his serious tone, mischief sparkled in Kevin's eyes as he reached for the door handle of the store. "Let's find out what Atherton has to hide."

5

56 Down; 5 Letters;
Clue: Move. Change gears.
Answer: Shift.

The wine store was better dressed than any of my apartments had ever been. A seating with leather chairs. Rows of gleaming bottles with multicolored labels. Stacks of wooden cases displayed various vintages.

Kevin eyed the shelves with a discerning gaze. He lingered over a bottle of red wine with a local label. "They have a good collection. A wide variety. Good décor."

"It's nice." My murmur of agreement brought a sideways glance. I fought to hide my laughter. "What do I know of fine wine? Or any wine?"

Kevin nodded in response to a clerk currently checking out another couple's purchase. "You can smell intrigue in the air, but not the aroma of a good wine."

My gaze scanned the aisles and corners. One woman was emptying a small crate of bottles. A slim man stopped her for a whispered consultation.

I tugged on Kevin's hand. "Bruce said his office is in the rear of the store."

Kevin and I strolled toward the corner where the man and woman stood.

As we approached the man looked up with a slight smile on his face. His gaze narrowed. Touching his co-worker's arm, he walked toward us. "You're Tracy Belden."

I started in surprise. Kevin, unlike me, kept his composure. No one other than Warren Kitt was supposed to know I was coming. "I am, but how do you know my name?"

"Bruce is expecting you." The words came with a sigh and an easing of the tension in the man's face. George, according to his nametag, gave a slight smile.

George included Kevin as he turned and waved a hand toward a corridor in the back corner. "His office is this way."

With my suspicions on full alert, I followed him. "Did Bruce discuss my arrival with his former partners?"

"I don't know. Bruce didn't tell me anything. I saw a Vegas news outlet on his computer with your picture." George slowed and glanced at us with a look of anticipation. "Are you buyers from one of the Vegas casinos? That would be amazing."

I answered with a smile and a wink. Best to play it cool, since I was completely confused. Either someone had blabbed or Pam had a major leak in her organization. Or perhaps the multiple audits had lit a fire under a guilty conscience.

The short hallway to the office left little time to ponder. The man rapped his knuckles on a closed door at the end of the hall. "Bruce? Tracy Belden's here."

No answer came.

George smiled apologetically. "I know he's here. I spoke with him an hour ago when someone called for him."

"We'll go in." The clerk spoke with a lilt in his tone. "I know he's waiting for you."

Part of me wanted to hold back, which was silly since I'd specifically arranged this confrontation. Perhaps the tension tap dancing up my spine accounted for my hesitation.

"Bruce?" George opened the door to a small office. "Tracy Belden's here."

Images flashed on my brain: A small desk by the window, paperwork piled on a spare chair, three crates of wine from different companies stacked by the front corner. A man sitting behind the desk faced the lone window in the room. A wine bottle and a glass with the dregs of a red liquid reflected the sunlight.

And the stillness.

The closed-in silence smacked me in the face. I tensed instantly. I heard nothing from Kevin. Not even the sharp intake of breath that gave evidence of my own shock. However, I felt his hand touch mine.

"Bruce?" George's voice sharpened. "Hey, bud. Wake up! You have visitors!"

When the clerk started forward, I grabbed his arm, forcibly holding him back. I returned his puzzled look with a stern one of my own. "I'll check on him."

Pushing him toward Kevin, I walked forward.

"What's going on?" George's confused tone gave no indication of alarm. "I can't believe he dosed off."

Two strides was all it took to put me behind the desk. Bruce Atherton's blank eyes stared at the blue sky outside above a slack jaw. His loose hands lay in his lap. He'd been thirty-two. A few years younger than me.

No pulse. No breath.

I looked at Kevin and shook my head. He already had his phone in his hand. He gave a nod and gently grabbed George's arm.

The clerk's wide eyes shifted from me to Kevin, fighting against my hubby's grip. "No! What are you doing? He's fine. He's napping. Does she think he's dead? Bruce can't be dead."

Actually, he can be, my brain answered irreverently. And he is dead.

As they turned to leave, I leaned over and smelled the dead man's mouth. The only aroma I could discern was sour wine. Using the back of my finger, I tipped the remaining liquid in the glass. No obvious residue, but it was a red wine. The laptop was closed. No notes on his desk. Nothing in the inside pockets of his jacket.

Kevin and George stood in the hall. Kevin was still on the phone. George glared at me with growing confusion.

I put out my hands out and pasted on a puzzled expression.

"Next time, leave a clue," I muttered to the dead man before walking away.

When I joined them in the hall and shut the door behind me, Kevin raised his phone. "The police are on the way."

George stared around as if lost. "He's not really dead, is he? How is he dead?"

"I don't know." I'd come to investigate fraud and ended up with a dead body. Was it suicide? Why? He'd just taken a buyout. But who would murder him?

Someone with something to hide.

Kevin put a hand on the man's shoulder. "Wait here with Tracy. I'll meet the police."

I exchanged a nod with Kevin as he turned to the front of the store. His move put him face-to-face with two women barreling toward us.

A chubby blonde with short curly hair wore a frown. She was whispering to her companion. "... am I here? You said you'd talk to him."

Seeing us, she shot the clerk a flirtatious smile. "Hey, Georgie. Bruce is expecting us."

The taller brunette with a model thin figure scanned Kevin and I with a quick once over. "Consulting on setting up your wine cellar? Bruce is the best."

"Hey, Natalie." George put out a hand to block the brunette from sidling past us. He'd finally found his voice, though it was breathless. Then, he turned and nodded to the blonde. "Yvonne. They're buyers from a casino in Vegas."

I didn't bother to correct the man. I was too busy studying two of the other partners. Neither woman blinked at Kevin and my supposed roles. Nor did they show any flicker of recognizing me as George had.

The clerk remained in the middle of the hall. "You can't see Bruce."

Yvonne, the blonde, tightened her jaw in defiance.

Behind them, a police cruiser pulled up to the curb. No lights or sirens. Like Langsdale, Nevada, the resort town where I lived, police don't like to alarm the tourists. They wouldn't believe Atherton was dead until they saw the body for themselves.

"George." Natalie added a touch of steel to the man's name. "This is important. Obviously, his previous meeting is over."

She raised a brow in my direction.

Kevin, standing beside George, looked pleasant enough, but no way would either woman get past my husband, or me.

Stepping around Kevin, I took a breath and considered how to play my hand. "You need to speak with the police. There's been... an accident."

Both women stiffened at my words. Their quick, silent exchange of startled looks was interrupted as the chime sounded from the door. Turning around, Natalie and Yvonne gasped as a uniformed police officer walked into the wine store.

The white guy was fifty-something. Curly, light brown hair had escaped from his cap. His wide build showed the beginning of a belly, but his quick gaze was intent and sharp. After a quick scan of the shop, he zeroed in on the five of us clogging the corridor. He nodded to his right before striding toward us.

After a cursory look at the three locals, the man locked in on me and Kevin, ending with my husband. "Did you call 9-1-1?"

"I did, officer. I'm Kevin Tanner." Kevin moved to one side of the narrow hall and pointed to the door at the back of the hall. "He's in there."

"Wait a minute." Natalie's strident tone betrayed the uncertainty in her eyes. She evidently disliked not having all the facts. "I demand to know what's going on. Why have the police been called? What happened to Bruce?"

Yvonne's face was pinched with worry. "Is Bruce going to be okay?"

Fear bordering on panic threaded through her voice, as she registered the arrival of the police rather than an ambulance.

I held out a hand to Officer Clark, per his nametag. "Perhaps we should all wait in an empty office if one is available?"

George pointed wordlessly to a closed door slightly behind us.

Kevin stepped back and opened the door. A small table with four chairs was offset with a set of shelves and various brochures.

Officer Clark quickly seized control. "Everyone wait in here. No talking until I get back. Don't call anyone. George, come with me."

The wine clerk tensed instantly. Too bad Clark hadn't asked me. I wouldn't have minded another look at the scene.

Being in the room with the two woman was like being caged with a pair of wild-eyed tigers. No one sat except Kevin, who took the chair farthest from the door. I was too busy studying the other women.

Yvonne stood with a hand over her mouth, leaving only her scared, worried gaze flickering back and forth.

"He can't keep us here." Natalie got in Yvonne's face so quickly, her long, straight hair swung out behind her. She swiveled to face Kevin and me. "Who are you two? How do you know Bruce?"

"I'm Tracy Belden." Pause for recognition. Again, not a flicker at hearing my name. "This is my husband, Kevin Tanner. As George said, we flew in from Vegas. We came to speak with Bruce."

"Did you?" Yvonne demanded. With her fists clenched by her chest, she looked like an angry pixie. "What have you done?"

The door opened before I could answer. Officer Clark's solemn expression confirmed what Kevin and I already knew. His demeanor put the other two women on alert. Both tensed like tightly strung wires.

He met their eyes with a sympathetic look. "Bruce is dead."

Their exclamations of sorrow and shock appeared genuine. Both gasped. I didn't have to look at Kevin to know his intense gaze was studying them as well.

Yvonne collapsed in a chair. Burying her head in her hands, her shoulders shook.

Natalie put a hand to her chest as if she'd been struck with a lance. After the denials that it must be a mistake, the woman turned toward the outsiders. Her gaze slid by Kevin's sympathetic expression to land on me. "Bruce was fine when I spoke with him this morning. What did you say to him? What have you done?"

They'd talked this morning? Yet she didn't know my name and Bruce had. Interesting. I met her gaze and shook my head. "We never met him. George led us back to the office. When we found him, Bruce was already dead. It was right before you came in. You said you had an appointment with him also?"

"No." Yvonne raised her head, wiping at her eyes. Her lip quivered as she spoke. She took a trembling breath. "We just dropped in."

Natalie opened her mouth. Her body tensed. Her narrowed eyes pierced her friend with a hard look.

Cautioning her to silence?

Officer Clark studied all four of us equally. "The lieutenant's on his way. The coroner's been called."

Deadwood's population of fourteen hundred people coupled with its low crime rate, including zero murders for the last year, meant there was no homicide detective. There was simply no need. The police force of less than twenty officers would handle the investigation.

I kept my gaze on the other two women. "Bruce called and asked you to come here."

Yvonne nodded. Her gaze slid sideways to me. Then, she tensed.

Natalie's expression tightened. "You have no right to ask questions of us."

I shrugged at her rising ire. "The telephone records will prove who called who, as well as the timeline."

Clark eyed Kevin and I with an intense gaze. "Let me see your I.D.s. George said you were wine buyers from a casino in Las Vegas. Who do you work for?"

Exchanging a look with Kevin, I reached in my bag. Should I speak with the police officer privately? Or come clean now? In a town this size, the truth would ripple through the streets within moments. Best to see the women's reactions in person.

I held out my wallet to Clark. "George made an assumption regarding my business with Mr. Atherton. I'm a private investigator from Langsdale, Nevada. I'm here on a case."

Clark stiffened but didn't stop. He studied my Nevada P.I. license and made a few notations in his small notebook before handing it back. His eyes narrowed at seeing Kevin's driver's license. "You're her partner?"

Kevin shrugged. "In a manner of speaking. I'm her husband. I'm just along for the ride and to see Deadwood. It's a lovely town."

My brain came up with a comment about eye candy. The smart aleck quip was on my lips, but I managed to clamp my jaw shut. I'd alienated a few police officers in Nevada. With no Crawford on-site to bail me out, I figured I should play nice for now.

I hadn't even bothered to check whether my P.I. license was reciprocal in South Dakota. My report on possible fraud would have gone straight to Crawford, then Pam Isley. I'd never expected to be involved in a death, whether it was suicide or possible murder.

Clark handed back our I.D.s. He loomed over us, not giving an inch. "What exactly are you investigating that involves... involved Bruce Atherton?"

I raised my chin and looked him in the eye. "I'd rather not go into detail without contacting my client."

Yvonne groaned. "It's the buyout. Of course."

"Yvonne!" Natalie turned on her friend. Her raised fists were clenched. "Keep quiet!"

"Oh, please, Natalie!" The other woman struck the table with her open hand in the first show of defiance since they'd arrived. "Everyone is town already know. Why else would a P.I. be here? Pam Isley is doing another on-site review. Did you think they'd hand over this much money without due diligence?"

Clark had watched the women during the outburst. He turned to me with a raised brow.

Still digesting the scene, I nodded. "That's pretty much it."

"Good to know." A new player filled the open doorway, closing it behind him. A white guy with a solid build, high cheek bones and light brown hair, he looked to be in his mid-forties. Brown eyes flashed above a nose that had been broken more than once. He nodded a greeting to Clark, then surveyed the rest of us. "I'm Lieutenant Lawrence Hawken. I'll be looking into Bruce Atherton's death."

Clark jerked his head toward the end of the hall. "Phillips and Lloyd are taking pictures. They're bagging everything, including the bottle of wine and the glass. I closed off the office. George is in the next office. The coroner is waiting for you before she moves the body."

"Good." Hawkens nodded approval. His gaze touched briefly on the rest of us as his hand moved toward the doorknob. "I'll be back in a few minutes."

The closing of the door seemed to mark a new chapter. The police investigation had officially begun. My own case had taken a darker turn. With no signs of violence on the body, Bruce Atherton had almost certainly been poisoned.

Was it by his own hand? Or had someone wanted to silence him before he spoke with me?

6

26 Across; 5 Letters;
Clue: Friends. Partners.
Answer: Mates.

I wanted more than anything to confer with Kevin. However, under the eagle eyes of Officer Clark, that was impossible. I settled for sitting next to him at the small table and holding his hand.

My hubby was on one side of the table, within arm's length of Yvonne. Despite the woman's stunned expression and downcast gaze, her eyes were alert.

Natalie stalked the narrow end of the room. She spun suddenly and pointed at me. "You did this! You're responsible for his death!"

Being an outsider, I took her accusation in stride. However, I noted she didn't accuse Kevin.

"Natalie." Clark voice was calm yet stern. He walked toward her. "Everyone's in shock. You're distraught. Sit down and try to relax. Hawk will talk to each of you in turn. Until then, I'll have some water or coffee brought in."

Knowing how long questioning by the police could take when a dead body was involved, I squeezed Kevin's hand. "At least we ate at Legends before coming here."

Diverted by Natalie's outburst, Clark hadn't noticed my comment. The woman finally sat. Unfortunately, she was directly opposite me and continued to stare daggers at me.

Clark diverted her attention by asking about Atherton's next of kin.

I continued to study Natalie. Her hostility seemed out of proportion considering Yvonne's reaction. Misplaced guilt, perhaps?

The door opened on my musings. Hawkens stepped inside. Clark held up his notebook and explained about the contact information for the family.

"Good." Hawkens nodded. "I've arranged for water and coffee to be brought. I'll need to speak with each of you. There's another room down the hall. Officer Clark will remain here. I'll start with Ms. Belden and Mr. Tanner together."

Kevin and I followed him down the narrow hall. I caught a glimpse of George in the main part of the store. Another police officer and the female clerk we'd seen initially stood with him. He met my gaze with an angry frown. Probably annoyed I hadn't corrected his assumption.

The exchange lasted only seconds before Hawkens opened the door to an even smaller office. A narrow desk filled one corner. File cabinets and shelves of binders covered the walls. One wheeled office chair faced two straight backed chairs. Kevin and I sat side-by-side facing Hawkins.

"The Isley Corporation hired you." After a glance at Kevin, Hawkens addressed me. "Warren Kitt has been working with the Prairie Sun and Spirits for months."

The accuracy of the rumor mill in Deadwood didn't surprise me. I'd grown up in a small town. "The buyout is a done deal. Everyone in town must know about it. Do you know why Natalie and Yvonne argued about keeping a lid on it?"

He shook his head, silently studying me.

I returned his gaze. "Is there any indication if it's suicide or murder? I see no motive for either."

His tense expression relaxed slightly. He leaned back in the chair. "Nothing obvious. Bruce and three of the other partners were well known. They've been in the area for almost five years. One, Tom Hayden worked remotely. Tell me, exactly what are you here to investigate?"

Pam Isley already didn't like me. I wasn't going to blab. "I can't tell you that without speaking with my client."

Hawken's mouth tipped up ever so slightly. "The accountants found a problem with the records. They're trying to close the barn doors after the horse is out by sending you here. Bruce and Tom Hayden both received the buyout."

Despite his on-point guess, I kept my mask in place.

"Don't bother denying it." He waved a hand as I opened my mouth to repeat my disclaimer. "Who knew you'd been hired? How did Bruce find out? Natalie and Yvonne didn't know."

I threw my hands up. "I've been wondering about Bruce's source of information since George greeted me by name. Only Pam Isley and Warren Kitt were supposed to know. There have been e-mails back and forth, but-"

A bell rang in my brain. "Records. Computer programs."

Kevin met my gaze. An answering light sparked in his eyes. He faced Hawkens. "Yvonne was the computer wizard. Who did most of the actual work on the computer?"

The police lieutenant hesitated only briefly. "Bruce."

I ran through the scenario. "Yvonne created the program the company used, but Bruce worked it. When Warren was made CEO after the buyout, he was given a sign-on to the Prairie Sun and Spirits program."

Hawkens smiled at my logic chain. "Bruce traced the e-mails regarding your hire. Why not tell the others?"

"That could be why Natalie and Yvonne were here." As I spoke several questions appeared on my list of clues. "I was contacted two days ago. Travel plans were finalized yesterday. Bruce couldn't have known for long. What did he tell George?"

A buzzing sounded from both Kevin's and my phone.

Kevin glanced at the readout before smiling at me. "I'm surprised it took this long."

I chuckled until I saw Hawken's expression stiffen. "Our son came with us. He's at the shootout with some family friends. He's a twelve-year-old Sherlock Holmes."

Hawken grunted. "Deadwood's grapevine is alive and well."

Kevin shook his phone. "Can I assure him we're not dead?"

"I think that's safe." Hawken expression turned serious. "As for George, he saw your picture on Bruce's laptop. Bruce shut it immediately and said you'd be stopping in and to watch for you."

I leaned forward. The timing of Bruce's death was too close to my arrival not to be suspicious. "Did Bruce see anyone else today? Did he receive any calls?"

After an assessing look, the police lieutenant rubbed a hand over his face. "After speaking with George, I checked Bruce's computer history."

A jolt shot through me. "His computer wasn't locked?"

Hawken shook his head. "An officer found the laptop in a partially open desk drawer. His search history brought up a few articles regarding your cases over the last few months."

When I groaned, Kevin nudged my arm. His over-wide grin matched his teasing expression. "You're a star."

Hawken chuckled. "You have an impressive record, Ms. Belden."

"Call me Tracy. The truth is: I like to solve puzzles, and I'm good at it. That's my main qualification."

Hawken nodded. "I don't remember the last time we had a murder in Deadwood. I'm happy for any help you can give me. I don't have the records for the office phone. Bruce's cell showed multiple calls to and from Tom Hayden today."

"The other buyout." Kevin noted as his fingers tapped his thigh. "Now on the North Carolina coast."

"At last report," I muttered. When Hawken stiffened, I waved a hand at the enigmatic look in his eyes. "I've learned to verify everything."

Kevin snorted. "Miss Marple warned Belden that people lie."

Hawken snorted at the name of the fictional sleuth. "Excellent advice. Why would Tom be the person Bruce called rather than his friends in town? I'll contact the local police. If they confirm Hayden is there, they can talk with him."

"Let me know what you find out." I grimaced at another buzzing from my phone and Kevin's. "The wine cork was on the table. A third of the wine was gone. The date on the bottle was early twentieth century. Does the store carry that vintage?"

"No." Kevin's no-nonsense reply came before the lieutenant opened his mouth. My hubby's self-deprecating expression was by way of an apology. "That's a rare vintage. Sixty known bottles in the world. High five figures."

"He's a man of many talents." I explained to Hawken's stunned expression. "Raised in Europe."

"I see." The police officer recovered his composure. "You two make an interesting pair. I'll ask Natalie and Yvonne about the bottle. It and the glass will be tested. There's no sign of a visitor. The other three employees say he was alone for the last hour."

"Back door?" I asked. There had to be one for deliveries.

Hawken nodded. "He could have let someone in. Which would explain the amount of wine that's missing."

Kevin flipped a gold dollar over his knuckles. "Or he was working up his courage by enjoying the rare vintage, before..."

The lieutenant looked thoughtful. "Possible. I'll have to wait for the autopsy to confirm cause of death. It might have been a heart attack or a stroke."

We three exchanged skeptical looks.

Hawken sighed. "We'll know more once the lab completes the tests. George watched Bruce open the bottle. How would someone add poison to a closed bottle?"

"Another question to add to the list." They were piling up. "I wonder what secret is out there that's worth killing for."

7

33 Across; 8 Letters;
Clue: Where things join.
Answer: Juncture.

Marcus's exuberant energy from Monday evening hadn't abated by Tuesday morning. Our discussion of the case last evening had been interspersed with a retelling of the gunslinger shootout. At the moment, after starting the dishwasher, I was nursing a second cup of coffee.

Mrs. C had resurrected her knitting needles and yarn. Her latest project was a set of shawls for the ladies in her reading group. Since they were currently watching our two newly acquired felines, Kevin and I had popped for the yarn. The older woman eyed me with a placid expression that left me wary. "What's your next step, eh, ducks? Having a dead body in the mix complicates the matter, I'd say."

I took a sip of the dark roasted coffee, savoring the heat before nodding. "Pam and Crawford agreed with you. Neither was happy about the news. Although I don't think it's fair for them to blame me for the man's death."

Kevin sat down at the table with a carrot cake muffin in one hand and a fresh cup of coffee in the other. "Hawken should have a preliminary autopsy report today, along with the results on the wine."

"That should answer a few questions." I stared across my coffee cup while inhaling the tantalizing aroma. "My next goal is to talk with Matt Crocker. Other than Hayden, Crocker is the last main player I haven't-"

A high-pitched scream cut me off.

I gasped and jostled my cup. Fortunately, I escaped scalded fingers. "I'm assuming that's not Rabi."

"Look what I found!" Marcus's scream drug out the last word as he ran through the house. He skidded to a stop in the wide arch connecting the dining and living rooms. He held a whiteboard out for all to see. "Ta-da!"

Rabi followed him in at a far more sedate pace. He brandished a handful of markers and a small smile.

I put a hand over my heart. This boy and his melodrama might be the death of me. "Good grief."

Marcus was already clearing off the top of the bureau with Kevin's help. I cringed at the boy's hurried handling of the decorative items. Fortunately, Kevin rescued them before any damage was done.

"People! People!" Marcus threw his hands up in the air. He looked like a preacher addressing his congregation. I almost threw in a Hallelujah, but I didn't want to get in trouble. The boy child waved several colored pages in the air. "I printed off photos of the people involved."

Wanting to do my part, I headed for the kitchen. "I'll get tape for the pictures."

Moments later, Marcus faced his audience. "This is an official meeting of the Belden-Tanner Detective Agency. We are here to discuss the Case of the Purloined Profits."

"Purloined?" Kevin questioned. "That means stolen. The problem is too *much* money."

"Allegedly." Marcus pounced on Kevin's comment. "If they have extra money, it had to come from somewhere. Every one of us mentioned having too much cash makes no sense."

I frowned. "Rabi never actually said that."

My son stabbed a marker at me. "He thought it! Didn't you? And no rabble rousing in the meeting!"

Rabi nodded, a twinkle in his eye softened his stern looks.

Kevin pointedly moved his cup farther away from me. "If you can't behave, I'm moving seats."

I gently kicked his leg at his snarky comment. "Where did you get a photo of Hayden and Matt Crocker? Bruce and the two women are on social media, but the company web-site only has avatars for the five partners."

"I had to dig." Marcus busily wrote the names and titles of the principles, adding Warren Kitt to the lineup. "I found a group picture from college."

The last photo he put up showed the five partners smiling for the camera. Two dark haired men of medium build, Crocker and Hayden, bookended the group with Atherton in the middle.

"It's hard to tell them apart from here." A red lettered 'dead' was written above Bruce's photo. Under motive was written a single word: money. When I read it out loud, Marcus faced me, tossing the green marker up and down.

"Too much money led us here." The boy child narrowed his eyes. "Did you ever start a scam with extra cash on the books?"

He aimed the question at Kevin. My hubby was the only one in the room who had any real experience with high finance.

Kevin's expression turned serious. "In scams you have to flaunt money to get money. We created our own accounts. We could have any amount of cash we needed to grab the mark's attention."

"Get their attention." Discussing the facts out loud helped me see things clearer. "The Isley Corporation wouldn't have bought out the Prairie Sun and Spirits without confirming the bottom line."

The tapping of Mrs. C's knitting needles sounded in the silence. "The excess didn't present itself until after the purchase. Days, weeks afterward. The timing of the fraud and the man's death are highly suspicious."

Her words echoed in my mind. "Both events seem to be orchestrated. Who could do that?"

A spark lit up several of my synapses. I grabbed Kevin's arm, who, despite his threat, still sat beside me. "You padded your own accounts."

His eyes narrowed. His expression was watchful. "It's the easiest way to make yourself look rich."

Marcus laughed. "Have to have an inside man cook the books."

I froze as my mind's eye turned to my mental crossword puzzle which had stubbornly refused to come together. Suddenly, a portion of it rearranged and made some kind of sense.

I had one answer and an untold number of questions, but at least I was moving forward. "There's only one person who could have messed up the Prairie Sun and Spirits's books and gotten away with it. One person who forced this investigation: Warren Kitt."

Reactions varied from Kevin's agreement to Mrs. C's surprise.

"Why?" Marcus asked.

"I don't know." I'd dug heavily into the history of the five partners. I'd done some research on Kitt, but not as much. A mistake I planned to correct. "Kitt discovered the Prairie Sun and Spirits and brought it to Pam's attention. He orchestrated the background checks into the company and sat in on the negotiations for the purchase."

Mrs. C was knitting like her needles were on steroids. "Why would he throw a monkey wrench into the works after the fact?"

Kevin rapped the table. "He couldn't have known Pam would send you."

"I wasn't the target." I waved my hand at his false assumption. "His false records drew attention to the company and to the partners. That was the only foreseeable outcome of his machinations."

Marcus finished circling Kitt's photo with several red circles. "Why?"

I went back to the basics. "The five partners met while attending the University of South Dakota. Neither Hayden nor Crocker graduated. They left school to concentrate on the company."

"The University of South Dakota?" Mrs. C stiffened. "I met a lovely lady yesterday who retired from there after thirty years. I'll be happy to check for any news related to your case."

"Anything would help." I could only find so much from the official channels. "The Prairie Sun and Spirits had a steady flow of money coming in before the sale. Yet they didn't show a major profit until after the business left their hands."

"Missing money?" Rabi's eyes hardened with a cynical look.

The others perked up, but I had to shake my head.

"All the grants and loans are accounted for." I hedged my defense with a knowing look. "At least on paper. The wines and beers got good reviews. Sales were slow, but steady. Atherton and Matt were the face of the company. They made the contacts and pushed the sales of the liquor."

Kevin leaned forward, setting his elbows on the table. "They were successful enough to get Isley's attention. Yet bad enough to sell the company. In a perfect scam, you need to get the money and get out before anyone knows they've been had. If you get greedy and stay too long, it's bad news."

"People get all kind of mad about being tricked." Marcus who'd been updating the board, turned. Though his tone was serious, his eyes were puzzled. "But how does blowing grant money tie into Kitt setting up the investigation? What did he think would happen?"

Mrs. C's knitting needles had stilled. "I'm not seeing the threads tie together either, luv."

I tapped the table as I poked at my crossword puzzle I'd built for this case. "I don't have all the answers, but I'm on to something. The puzzle says so, and the puzzle never lies, well not often, maybe sometimes. But not this time."

"Very reassuring." Mrs. C raised her brows. Her concern for my mental state was apparent. Her needles slowed as she cast me a sideways glance. "What would you have of us?"

"Arrghh!" I raked my hands through my hair. "We don't have our usual contacts here."

"Just remember one thing." Marcus left the security of the white-board and put his hand on my shoulder. His left hand gripped the blue marker. His expression was somber. "No matter what happens, we're not leaving until Friday."

I smacked the table and glared at the boy. "Why did I expect a serious response from you?"

He spread out his hands. "I *am* serious! There's cool stuff going on all week. More gunfights, a train from the eighteen-eighties, the Crazy Horse monument, and tons more."

I sucked in a breath. I could hardly blame the boy. We'd never been in this area. Gunfights, giant carved mountains. What more could a boy want? I put on my mom hat.

"Fear not." A chuckle accompanied my words. "We'll get to all of your planned activities. We don't fly out of Rapid City until Friday. What did you have planned-"

Marcus's loud gasp over-rode my words. "This is perfect!"

"-for today?" I finished my sentence despite the boy's outburst.

Mrs. C's nimble fingers paused as the boy turned to her, his eyes full of expectation. Their gazes met. Marcus's jabbing finger almost met the older woman's eye before her wrinkled brow cleared. "Oh course! That will work out like a treat, luv. Our trip must have been meant to be."

Thankfully, Kevin and Rabi looked as confused as I felt. "What trip?"

"Tour of the Prairie Sun and Spirits Brewery," Rabi inserted.

I put a hand to my forehead. "I forgot all about that. The Crockers and Yvonne live on-site. Matt should be there. Between the five of us, we can find a way for me to question him."

My hopes rise. A little more digging into the backgrounds of everyone involved should serve me well.

Marcus clapped his hands. "Even better... they have food."

Kevin gave the boy a thumb's up before winking at me. "You may also get another shot at Natalie and Yvonne. A trifecta!"

8

37 Down; 4 Letters;
Clue: Center of operations.
Answer: Base.

After several aborted discussions on the all important topic of where and when to eat, Marcus stated that for politeness's sake we should have an early lunch at the brewery's café.

His pretense of manners fooled no one. He wanted to pursue the case.

"I have to get something." He started to put down the markers. Then, he spun on his heel and pointed them at us like weapons. His narrowed eyes glared at each of us in turn. "Nobody touch the white board."

Mrs. C saluted him with her loose knitting needle. "I'll keep them in line, ducks."

I sipped my coffee and hoped Pam Isley never learned about our methods for solving cases.

After a few minutes of rustling from the other room, my errant son returned. With a triumphant smile on his face, he held up both hands. Cords and pieces of electric equipment peeked out from his clenched fists.

"Are those earbuds?" I asked.

He walked to the table. "And a mic and a receiver. You're wearing a wire."

I took a long drink of my coffee. "Why did you bring that stuff?"

The boy heaved a long-suffering sigh. "We're on a case, T.R. As detectives, we have to be prepared. How did you solve any cases on your own?"

Kevin, resting his chin in his hand, smirked. "I've often wondered that myself."

Aiming a mock glare at my smart aleck hubby, I focused on our son. "This tape may not be admissible in court if I don't tell them they're being recorded."

"Of course, don't tell them!" Marcus looked at me as if I were crazed. "This isn't for court. This is so the rest of us can be in on the kill. Although, South Dakota is a one-party state. So, the tape will be admissible in court. You have to make them confess."

"I'll do my best, but I doubt I'll get anything crucial." I added my own long sigh. "And I get the last of Mrs. C's homemade scones. I'm also going to need more coffee."

Several minutes later, the small mic was in place, and the receiver had been tested. The range was over one hundred yards. Marcus told me with a serious expression that he had invested in quality. Of course, he'd used my money to do it.

Kevin, herding us toward the car like cats, raised a brow. "Are we eating before or after Belden accuses one of them of murder?"

"Before." Mrs. C surprised tone left no room for argument. She clutched her smaller knitting bag. "Eating afterward would appear heartless, wouldn't it? We don't want that."

"Of course not." As if accusing someone of murder wouldn't seem heartless? My sarcasm was apparently lost on the older woman and Marcus. "Besides, we don't know it was murder. It might have been suicide or natural causes."

"It wasn't natural causes." Marcus snorted. He waved his hand without turning around. "And suicide still implies guilt."

A call on my cell phone saved me from agreeing. "It's Hawken. I wonder what's he got?"

"You were right." The lieutenant's serious tone returned my greeting. "Poison. Hemlock, which can be found in any meadow or ditch in South Dakota."

"Hemlock." I repeated the poison for the benefit of my audience. "Was it in the bottle, the glass, or both?"

"Both." His voice grew heavier. "If the poison was added to the bottle first, it was premeditated. How could the killer know only Bruce would drink it? It would have been injected through the cork. That's so damaged, there's no proof of anything."

"Unless Bruce or the murderer added it to the open bottle." I stroked my lip in thought. "Any word on what Hayden and Bruce discussed on the calls?"

A thud sounded over the line. Whether from Hawken smacking the desk or his boots hitting the floor was hard to tell. "I haven't found Hayden yet."

It took me only seconds to decipher the meaning behind his harsh tone. Surprised, I looked at Marcus, who was planted right in front of me. "Are you saying Hayden's in town?"

My son's eyes grew wide.

"Yes." Disgust mixed with anger in Hawken's tone. "I got a download from his cell phone. The location shows he was in the area of the main house by the brewery during all three calls. Natalie and Yvonne didn't mention they had a visitor."

I narrowed my gaze. "How long has he been in Deadwood?"

"Off and on for several days by the look of it." Hawken's increasing ire showed in his tone.

That didn't add up in a town the size of Deadwood. "It's odd no one mentioned seeing him: in town, at the brewery. Word should have gotten should."

No immediate answer came. "I hadn't thought of that. I doubt anyone in town would recognize him by sight. His family has tour boats on the coast of North Carolina."

And the questions kept multiplying in my puzzle. "He worked remotely the entire time. He received a full buyout at the sale. *Then,* he returns to town?"

Mrs. C cocked her head to one side. "Perhaps it was a visit for old time's sake?"

The gleam in Marcus's narrowed gaze spoke differently. "Or he wanted more money to keep secrets buried."

"This story doesn't add up." Hawken's determined voice rang in my ear. "I'm headed out to talk to Hayden myself. I'll see what he had to say about his calls to Bruce."

"You might see me there." Best to warn him of my intentions. "My family and I are headed to the brewery now. We're going on a tour and having a bite to eat."

From his chuckle, Hawk evidently didn't believe in my rampant curiosity about the process of making beer. "I'll look for you. Good luck to us both."

Marcus stomped his feet in excitement. "No one mentioned Hayden was in town! That's super suspicious. Let's go!"

Mrs. C tapped my arm. She had a smug look on her face. "I'll wait until we're in the car for my news."

My interest meter shot sky high. "You spoke with your friend at the college? Did she know this group?"

"Yes, to both." The woman's British accent rang out across the warm summer air, sounding distinctly out of place on the plains of South Dakota. "Rather intriguing."

I could barely wait for the car to pull out of the driveway before I turned around and demanded the full story.

Marcus sat in the middle of the backseat with Rabi on the passenger side behind me. The man's dark eyes didn't share the sparkle of interest that covered my son's expression.

"There are several key points." Mrs. C settled her traveling knitting bag on her lap. "Mrs. Stone worked in the Young Entrepreneurs Department, which assisted students endeavoring to begin their own companies. That's where the five students coalesced as it were during their junior year."

Kevin gave a nod. "I wondered how they came together."

"Atherton had already started his business selling rare wines," the older woman went on. "Natalie and Tom Hayden were developing plans for an international computer company with Yvonne."

That tidbit caught my attention. "Natalie and Hayden."

Mrs. C sat back. Pleased with the effect of her bombshell. "The two had been an item all through college. Yvonne was dabbling her toes with no solid plans."

Marcus had followed the narrative closely. "Yvonne was dating Crocker first, right?"

"Mrs. Stone confirmed their romance." The older woman warmed to her tale. "Bruce introduced the pair. He and Matt had spoken of a partnership. Matt had no drive to start a company. What he had, *unlike the other four*, was capitol from an upcoming Mason Family Trust fund."

She paused expectantly.

The name rang a bell, but my brain was busy organizing several clues. "Are you saying Matt Crocker funded the whole thing with his inheritance?"

"Exactly." Mrs. C's grin looked like the Cheshire Cat's. Her red tipped nail stabbed the air, underlining her words. "Without Crocker's money, there would have been no Prairie Sun and Spirits."

"And no eventual buyout," I muttered.

Marcus poked Mrs. C's arm. "When did Natalie and Matt get together?"

"Shortly before his twenty-first birthday, which was when he received access to the trust." Mrs. C's cynical tone belied any romantic notion.

"Love at the first sight of his money." After delivering his judgement, Marcus laughed along with the rest of us. "Yvonne was left out in the cold."

Kevin glanced at me, a grin on his lips. "Neither of us had to worry the other was marrying for money."

"Not hardly." I chuckled. Our marriage of a few weeks ago had brought us a sliver of breathing room after Kevin moved into my and Marcus's loft apartment. That, my P.I. paychecks, and our fledgling handyman business was all that was keeping us off the streets.

I faced the front of the car. While my gaze absently watched the scenery of South Dakota stretch away to the horizon, my brain took note of the tangled relationships the group had built their company on.

"It lasted most of five years." Longer than I would have thought considering the usually volatile nature of broken romances.

I had a few more pieces to my puzzle and far more questions. However, my black-and-white grid was mostly empty. I was so preoccupied, I didn't realize we'd arrived until Kevin drove through the wooden gates of the Prairie Sun and Spirits' brewery on the city limits.

The scenic landscaping coupled with the stone patio of umbrella covered tables could have been in the English countryside. The situation would have been more enjoyable if I hadn't been hunting a killer.

As Kevin turned off the car, he faced me. "They have a bar and grill in the city. Your quarry might be there."

Why question the decision now? Was he testing me? "Hayden's hiding out. He's not in town, and neither are the others. Bruce's death is a perfect excuse for them to lay low."

Cozy looking stone worked buildings made an idyllic scene. Several tables were filled with couples or groups of friends. A soft breeze stirred the leaves. A rustic sign with an overflowing mug and an open wine bottle swung over the wide door leading to an open tavern.

My gaze lingered on the sign.

Kevin followed my line of vision. "What are you thinking?"

I shifted closer to him, though only the five of us were on the path toward the tables. "I'm thinking there's more than one way to get poison into a bottle of wine."

Marcus, who'd followed our conversation from behind us, pushed between us. "Why would the killer put the poison in the bottle after it was open?"

"To create confusion." Which I had aplenty in this case. "If the poison was only in the glass, the killer had to be present the day Bruce died. If it's in the bottle..."

Marcus jumped on my open-ended comment. "The police have to trace who had access to the bottle. All the killer had to do was wash their glass and put it back. You're good at being sneaky, T.R."

"Thanks, I think." Impatience boiled inside of me at the chance to waylay Matt Crocker and Tom Hayden. I dragged my feet. For once my stomach was over-ridden. "I'm going to the main house. I can't sit here."

Kevin kissed my cheek and stepped away. "Okay."

"That's it?" I eyed him suspiciously. "No protests about facing a possible killer alone? Just, see you later?"

He gave me his best innocent look. "You can pretend you're going off alone, and we'll pretend Rabi's not going to show up at the first sign of trouble."

I chuckled. "Deal. At least Hawken should be there as back-up."

I walked back and took the fork in the path. The others walked toward the patio. Other than a couple of signs warning me not to go this way, nothing stood in my way. High hedges and a row of trees gave way to a low built ranch house to one side and a two-story cottage on the other side. Each structure had a two-car garage.

Despite space for several cars to park, there was no sign of a police cruiser. Hawken would surely have used an official vehicle. Perhaps he'd been delayed. After a moment, I opted to try the ranch house. Rather than the front door, I slipped around the side.

The murmur of voices carried easily on the still air. Most people fail to appreciate how far a conversation can be heard, especially out in the country with no traffic sounds to mask the words. I slowed my steps.

"I didn't see him that morning!" The man's voice sounded desperate and trapped. No telling if it was Hayden or Crocker. "*You* drove in to talk to him."

"I was delayed!" Natalie's composed tone seemed a little patronizing. "How could you not warn me about the private detective? What does Pam Isley know? What does the Belden woman know?"

Not as much as I'd like.

"Stop it! Both of you!" Yvonne's guttural tone joined the fray. Her stern voice teetered on hysteria, but her command brought silence. "We have to pull ourselves together. Lieutenant Hawken will be here soon. He must have the cause of death by now. Obviously, Bruce committed suicide. None of us would have killed him."

That sounded rather naïve and certainly more hopeful than realistic. Who else knew him well enough to murder him?

"She's right." The man was obviously speaking to Natalie. "We have to stick to the same story. Bruce was depressed. He kept his feelings hidden from everyone."

"Bruce?" Yvonne's astonished tone put a lie to the story. "He's been complaining about the set up non-stop from day one."

I did a quick look around the area at my back, but saw no one. If I got caught, I could come up with an excuse. No way would this group be this forthcoming under direct questioning. Obviously, they had plenty to hide.

"We're so close to making this work." Natalie's voice broke on the last word. Unlike her competent pose yesterday, the woman had turned into a doomsayer. Her nerve was breaking. "After all this time."

Neither Kevin nor Rabi would have anything but disdain for her lack of composure in the face of a crisis. Even Marcus and Mrs. C would have faced a catastrophe with more resolve.

"Natalie!" Yvonne's voice was filled with anger. A high-pitched yelp of fear mixed with her exclamation.

A quick glance through the window showed the blonde gripping her friend's arms. I slipped out of sight rather than risk being seen.

"Listen to me." Blonde Yvonne sounded like she was about to blow a fuse. "I didn't come this far to fail now because you lost your nerve! This was your idea from the beginning. This whole thing is your fault! Both of you!"

Another quick glimpse showed the man-Matt Crocker? I couldn't tell from this angle. Crocker and Hayden's coloring was almost identical, and I only had Hayden's college photo to go on. Either way the man forced his bulk between the two women. He had to pry Yvonne away from the model-like brunette.

"We can make this work!" The man fought to maintain a calm tone.

Yvonne raked her hands through her short blond curls. "Talk to your wife. This sandcastle is built on a lie. You two talked me into this scheme. I'm not going to watch it crumble because you chicken out at the eleventh hour."

Keeping my body close to the wall, I risked another look. This was like watching a live action soap opera. What stunning revelation would come next? Fortunately, their actions had turned their faces away from where I stood.

Where was Hayden? Evidently not in the main house, but would he remain in the cabin at this crucial juncture? I looked at the other building, but saw no signs of life. Could Hayden have killed Bruce? Had Bruce, like Natalie lost his nerve within sight of the finish line?

They obviously wanted the final, ninety-day payout. However, I still wasn't sure what their secret was. If Lieutenant Hawken delayed long enough, I might learn the full story without any more detecting. I turned my attention to the unfolding drama.

Yvonne had retreated a few steps after her confrontation with Natalie.

Matt put a hand around his wife's shoulders. Cupping her face, he looked into her eyes. "We just have to get through the next few days. If we present a united front, there's nothing the police or that nosy P.I. can prove."

Natalie's tense shoulders relaxed. She wiped her hands across her face before straightening.

He shifted to get Yvonne's buy in to the new strategy.

The screech of tires on gravel had me spinning around as I tried to be one with the side of the house. No one driving up to the front could see me from here, but tell that to my rapidly beating heart.

"That must be Hawken." Natalie took the words right out of my mouth. With the windows open, the sound carried easily into the house.

Fortunately for them, the police officer had arrived during a lull in the screaming match.

"Listen!" Matt's voice was low and stern. "Bruce always had issues with depression. We thought he'd put it behind him, but he talked recently of not deserving our good fortune."

Yvonne had her arms crossed over her chest. "That's true enough."

Her enigmatic words stuck in my brain. What could she mean? They'd developed their business from the ground up. They'd sold it after a full audit. Yet, Warren Kitt had stumbled on a sticking point during his work with their company. Why hadn't he exposed them? Would Pam Isley have been liable after the purchase?

I couldn't make sense of their dilemma, but I had yet another question at the top of my list.

A car door slammed out front. Footsteps crunched on the gravel.

"Fine!" Yvonne threw up her hands at Matt's dark look. "I'll go along with the party line."

"So will I." Natalie's stiff voice sounded more like her tone from yesterday. "I lost control for a minute. We can get through as we have before. It's just us now."

A spike of alarm rang in my brain. Had Hayden skipped town? Or had he had to be silenced as well? Either would explain his absence.

Hawken's sharp rap on the door echoed through the house.

"I'll get the door." Matt's voice sounded through the window.

I inched my way toward the front of the house. I'd have to time my retreat carefully. The two men exchanged greetings. Waiting until the front door closed, I made sure no one was in sight. Fortunately, the women had remained in the seating area off the kitchen. So, the man headed toward the middle of the house.

Once I hurried to the gravel drive, it was a simple matter to turn and walk up the main path. I retraced Hawken's actions and climbed the few stairs to knock on the front door.

Yvonne opened the door just wide enough to block the entry path with her body. She greeted me with a stiff, harried gaze. "Ms. Belden, Lieutenant Hawken said you might be arriving. This is obviously not a good time. We'll speak with you-"

She raised her hand in front of her body, palm out and started to back up, closing the door in my face.

I almost laughed. If she thought telling me to leave was all it took to get rid of me, she quickly learned how wrong she was. I stiff armed the door open and thrust my body forward. Stepping into the house, I followed her as she retreated into the open living room.

Fury exploded in her eyes as a red flush colored her face. All her anger at her partners found a release. "How dare you! You have no right to push your way in here. You rude, intrusive bit-!"

"Why don't you call the police?" I thrust myself into her face. Satisfaction spread through me as the words stopped her cold. I stepped back before pointing behind her. "Hawken is in your sitting room. It'll be a short trip. Better yet, let's go talk to him together."

The dark flush on her neck only increased. She was practically seething with fury, but there was nowhere for her to go. She raised a clawed hand toward my face, ready and willing to strike out at someone.

I took a deep breath and relaxed my confrontational stance. "This situation isn't of my making, Yvonne. You and your friends started this."

She stiffened. Her anger melted away as she retreated half a step. Blinking rapidly, she pressed her lips together.

"The scheme was going to unravel at some point." I paused to let the words sink in. "Reality just caught up with you. Now, shall we join the others?"

I gestured to where the others waited. She made no move, but turned willingly when I put a hand on her elbow.

Hawken nodded to me at our entrance. "I thought that would be you. I'm surprised you didn't beat me here."

I decided now wasn't the time to mention I'd been listening at the open window for ten minutes. "My family's touring the brewery. I walked up."

Matt Crocker frowned. "This is private property. There are signs posted."

"And since the Isley Corporation hired me, I walked right past them." I watched his expression darken as the words sunk in. "You work for Pam Isley now. She sent me here to find answers. She won't stop until she's satisfied. Neither will I. It's the one thing we have in common."

The three remaining members of Prairie Sun and Spirits exchanged shuttered looks. Whatever their plan had been, the scheme seemed to be turning into quicksand beneath their feet.

I took advantage of the moment to study Matt Crocker. The forty pounds he'd gained since college rounded out his face, but something jarred with my memory. My brain refused to reconcile his college picture with the man before me. However, his profile showed the same broken nose from his photos.

Hawken stood by the window I had recently vacated. "I informed Bruce's friends of the cause of death. I've started tracing the sale of the wine to see who had access to it. The rest of the staff didn't record any other visitors."

Natalie put a hand on her husband's arm. Sorrow filled her eyes. "Bruce was prone to depression in college. Achieving his dream with the brewery put him on an even keel. But when sales didn't materialize and we had to sell, his depression returned worse than ever."

I fought to keep my expression neutral. Kevin can call up any emotion at a moment's notice. For some reason, knowing the tale was spun out of thin air, I was having a harder time than usual.

"Bruce fought against selling the brewery." Yvonne's soft notes held more truth than Natalie's. "He loved the business. It was all he wanted."

She opened her mouth as if to say more, but her voice seemed to drift away into memories.

Matt rubbed a hand over his face. "I can't believe he's gone. I never thought he would end his own life."

"There are several problems with a determination of suicide." Hawken watched each of them closely. His words drew everyone's attention. "If he killed himself, why was the poison in the bottle? He drank a third of the wine. He would have had symptoms long before drinking that much."

Natalie's eye narrowed. She put a hand over her heart. "You can't think someone murdered Bruce. Everyone loved him. There's no motive for anyone to kill him."

Her anguish and confusion sounded amazingly heartfelt. I had to admit, motive was the sticking point.

"Perhaps Tom Hayden could shed light on Bruce's state of mind." Hawken spoke quietly as he lobbed his grenade into the mix. "He's the one I came to speak with."

9

14 Across; 8 Letters;
Clue: Antagonistic manner.
Answer: Attitude.

From the stunned expressions of the three partners, the lieutenant's bombshell was more than satisfying. Stunned expressions. Guilty looks. Pale faces.

Natalie, recovering first, scoffed. "Tom's not here. He's in South Carolina with his family. You must know that."

The disbelief in her final words added just the right touch.

"I know Tom worked remotely the entire time. Then, he opted for the cash buyout along with Bruce." Hawken confirmed. "However, Bruce spoke with Hayden three times yesterday, and the location on Hayden's phone puts him in town. If anyone can shed light on Bruce's state of mind, Tom Hayden can."

You could have heard a pin drop. It's a cliché for a reason. The whole house seemed to hold its breath.

"That was me. I talked to Bruce yesterday." Matt seemed to jump at his own words. Shock gleamed in his eyes. "I can't believe I used Tom's phone."

Hawken simply stared at Matt.

The other man held out his hands. An apologetic smile touched his mouth. "I can explain. Tom and I got together when I traveled to South Carolina on a business trip. I just returned two days ago. When I left, I accidentally grabbed Tom's phone. He thought he lost it. I didn't realize I had it until last night. I'm the one who called Bruce. Tom was never in town."

Parts of the convoluted explanation struck me as true, but most of it had all the substance of cotton candy. The bottom line was: they couldn't produce Tom Hayden. The man seemed to be an integral part of the on-going mystery. At least they had Matt and his inheritance. As Mrs. C had said, where would they be without *that*?

Hawken's patent disbelief mirrored my feelings. The police officer pointed at Matt. "You called Bruce three times using the wrong phone."

"I used the one in my pocket." Matt shrugged as he returned Hawken's look. "I didn't realize it was Tom's. I called and told him this morning."

On the surface, the explanation sounded almost plausible, but these three had had years to... I frowned as my thought faded away in mid-sentence. Years to... what? Lie? Perfect their story?

I stepped back, literally and figuratively. When I lose my way in creating one of my crossword puzzles, getting an overall view of the whole usually puts me back on track. A crossword puzzle has to be symmetrical from top to bottom. All the clues and answers have to fit.

This puzzle, er case had too many clues that didn't flow together. Why did Warren Kitt cook the books to draw attention to the Prairie Sun and Spirits company after the sale was complete? Then, there was the Mason name cropping up with Matt and Warren. How did that tie in? The seemingly small detail was too coincidental not to be crucial. What was this nebulous scheme these three had touched on?

"What did you and Bruce discuss?" Hawken's carefully neutral tone brought me back to present.

The doorbell's chime interrupted any possible answer.

"Who could that be?" Natalie's strident tone matched the full-blown seething anger in her eyes.

"It's probably Warren Kitt." I raised my hand, then faced Hawken. "I may have forgotten to mention it, but I asked him to come. I think he can fill in the background. I'll get the door."

I didn't want Yvonne or the others to turn him away. A minute later, I escorted the Isley manager into the room. "I think you all know each other. You've been working together for months."

Then, like a perfect hostess, I introduced Warren to Hawken. Since I had the stage, I decided to throw a match into the volatile situation. I faced the police officer while pointing to Warren. "You see, Warren cooked the books on the Prairie Sun and Spirits' account just enough to draw Pam Isley's attention. He wanted to force an investigation into the partnership."

The collective gasps and outrage of the three partners was surpassed only by Warren's shock. His open mouth and wide eyes were picture perfect.

"What are you saying? I..." When he stared at me, I met his gaze with a knowing look. The tightness left his face, replaced with resignation. "How did you know? Not even the accountants caught it."

"Your expertise was your downfall." I admitted. "You're far too good not to have caught financial trouble in advance. Abnormally high sales could only have been manufactured from the inside, *after* you had access to their books. You should have been able to find the problem or dismiss it as nothing. If Pam trusted you less, she probably would have realized that fact."

Natalie stared at Warren with a hurt expression. "We've worked together for months. If you had a problem, why did you push the sale to begin with?"

Her dismay appeared to be genuine, and probably was.

Warren simply stared at her for a moment. "There was no problem with the initial sale. My siblings live in South Dakota. They're the only family I have left, and I wanted to relocate here. To justify the move, I needed to broaden the Isley interests in the area, and your company caught my interest."

Siblings. Family. All he had left. As my brain grabbed hold of his answers, an entire square of my crossword puzzle filled with answers. I sighed in relief. It's so nice when the answers fall in place.

Yvonne stared at him in growing confusion. "She said you messed up our accounts *after* the sale. Why?"

This time Warren couldn't come up with an answer.

I answered for him. "Once he was on the inside, he couldn't ignore the fact that something was off with your bottom line. Even I had to wonder how you could have so much money coming in from grants and loans yet *not* make a profit. You were selling green energy combined with wine and beer in a tourist mecca like Deadwood. During the first audit, he may have overlooked the dichotomy because he wanted to save your company."

Surprise and confusion showed on all of their faces.

I eyed Warren before continuing. This part of the picture was in focus now. "He's been tracking Matt's career for years. Haven't you, Warren?"

While the accountant looked surprised, Matt was totally freaked out.

Hawken was as taken aback as the others. "Why would he do that?"

"A common ancestor." I kept my gaze on Warren, who looked at me as if I had a rabbit in one hand and a top hat in the other. His lack of extended family had been the final clue I needed.

Yvonne appeared equally stunned. "How can you know that?"

Now I knew how Crawford, my boss man and a former police detective of twenty-five years, felt when I said dumb things. "You realize I'm an investigator, right? It's literally in my job title."

Hawken, more subdued, folded his arms over his chest. He zeroed in on me with a laser stare. "What's the connection?"

I pointed at Matt, who'd been strangely silent during my revelation. "Matt's money came from the Mason Family Trust. It was funded from a patent on a Mason gear commonly used in farm engines decades ago. Money poured in. The patent was sold. The name was changed. A trust fund was set up."

"We *know* that!" Natalie stomped her foot. She looked ready to launch herself at me.

I gave her a flat stare. "Did you know Warren's sister works at the Mason Family Grocery in Mitchell, South Dakota?"

Warren gasped. "You checked my family?"

I threw my hands in the air. "I verify what people tell me during my cases. This might surprise everyone except Hawken, but people sometimes lie during criminal investigations, especially ones involving *murder*."

My heavy dose of sarcasm drew a chuckle from Hawken. None of the others had a comeback. "When I investigate six people and find the name Mason connected to two of them, it makes me suspicious."

"Enough!" Matt closed the distance between us. "You're done. I'm not listening to your TV like summation for one more second!"

"Yes, you are." Hawken moved up to confront Matt. "She's working with the police in a possible murder investigation. You can listen to her here. Or we can all go the station, and you can listen to her there."

Matt glowered, but after a momentary stare down, he retreated.

Natalie put a hand on his shoulder, and the two stepped away together.

I still wasn't sure what plan these people had hatched, but the random details I'd learned over the last few days were finally coming together. And somewhere in my brain a picture was forming. If I could just put the clues in the right place.

Hawken nodded at me. "Go on."

"The other side of the equation begins with the partnership in college." I faced the trio with a sunny smile. "Natalie, Yvonne, and the missing Tom knew each other for years. Bruce had a fledgling business. He'd recently met Matt. They both loved old wines. They planned to go into business together, using the trust fund that was coming to Matt on his twenty-first birthday."

"Wait." Hawken's stiff tone cut across my scenario. "The grapevine said Yvonne introduced Matt to the others."

"Not according to the administrator of the program." I didn't add my theory that the rumor had been deliberately planted to mislead. "She remembered the players. Bruce and Matt had their business papers drawn up when the other three caught wind of their plans. Isn't that right, Matt?"

The man looked shell shocked. He swallowed hard and nodded. "Yeah, I knew Bruce first. Then, the others brought their skills to the mix. Bruce and I couldn't have done it without them."

"Sure, you could have." I scoffed at his disclaimer, ready to incite the masses. "Bruce was in business already. He had the expertise. You had money coming to you. People have made a success with much less. The others only had technical skills, which could be found anywhere."

"That's not true!" Yvonne leapt to her feet. "We were a team! Matt was all for the idea. He wanted to be part of something. He agreed. He was ready-"

She broke off abruptly. Her body seemed to lock in place.

Matt, who'd been dumbstruck at her diatribe, shook off his stupor. "Of course, I was. It all worked out for the best."

"Did it?" I turned to Warren who'd been following the scene with rabid interest. "You know how much money they started with and the grants they received. If you add in the contracts they have and their sales, how are their profits so low?"

"Excuse me?" Natalie stepped into the ring, ready to land a few blows. "A bad economy. Supply line disruption. We made mistakes. We invested too much into infrastructure and development. We kept trying."

"No, you kept getting money." I stabbed my finger in her direction. "That was your skill. That was your dream. Not hard work."

Hawken put out his arms to separate the combatants. As Natalie took a step back, the lieutenant looked at me. "What exactly are you implying, Tracy?"

"I arrived here at the house before you did. I listened outside the window while these three discussed how close they were to pulling off some... scheme." I waited for the eruption.

All three attacked me with such ferocity that I couldn't help but laugh at their communal outcry.

"Let's wrap this up, okay?" I out yelled them with a voice that would have carried to the paddocks on my parent's Kentucky horse ranch. "Because, while I might be wrong on a few details, this little meeting put the big picture in focus."

Wallace eyed me with a guarded, but hopeful look.

Hawken snapped his fingers and motioned them to silence.

I caught Wallace's attention. "Next week's final payoff is rather large I'm assuming."

He started at my words. "Pam told you that?"

"She didn't have to." My careless tone was at odds with his surprise. "If the amount wasn't sizeable, they'd be gone by now."

"Where would they go?" Wallace asked in a puzzled voice.

"Probably out of the country." I faced the three partners. "Their dream was about striking it rich. Bruce's business plan and Matt's money were all they needed as a cover. The only question is: How did the real Matt Crocker die?"

I locked eyes with Yvonne. She flinched instantly. As the other two drew breath to refute my claim, I held up my hand. "Don't bother. It's like Wallace cooking the books. Once you know the answer, it's obvious. I saw the resemblance between Matt and Tom in a college photo. Same height and weight. Similar coloring."

Eyeing me with matching stares, Natalie and Matt locked hands and stepped close to each other. Stiff with fear, they swallowed their ire.

I met Matt's gaze. "You had a nose job, a little work on Tom's drooping eyes. The weight gain masks your other features. Fortunately, Matt was an orphan with no close family. Your move to the other side of the state left any acquaintances behind."

"It can't be." Hawken's face went slack. He studied Matt, er, Tom with wide eyes. "All this time? Why?"

The police lieutenant rounded the sofa. Picking a pale Yvonne as the weak link, he loomed over her. "Tell me!"

His overbearing tone pointed to his fury at being played for a fool. I jumped as his tone reverberated off the walls. Yvonne looked ready to faint.

Hearing his loss of control, Hawken took a deep breath and stepped back. "Yvonne, what happened? Why did the rest of you kill the real Matt Crocker?"

"We didn't kill Matt!" Yvonne raised her tear stained face. She took a shaky gulp and swiped at her wet cheeks. "Everything was in place. Bruce and Matt were on board. Natalie and I would do the tech side. T-Tom was... is a born salesman."

Hawken looked at the other two partners. "What happened?"

Tom's jaw tightened. He met my gaze with a stare that melted in seconds. His shoulders slumped. "It was an accident. A stupid, careless curve in the road after we'd been drinking. Matt was the only one hurt. He died instantly."

"I'm confused." Warren pushed forward. His comment might have been laughable under other circumstances. "How did you get the money from the trust? The bankers would have known the real Matt Crocker."

"Matt died *before* his twenty-first birthday." My gaze swept over the trio. "The money was never his, but they were so close to their prize. They weren't going to let a little thing like a man's death stop them. Tom took his place when they met the lawyers. Tom and Matt both conveniently dropped out of college. No one saw the real Matt Crocker after that."

Tom gave a rueful chuckle before his expression drooped. "Eight days. Matt wanted us to have it. So, I changed my hair, wore glasses, grew a beard. They didn't even blink when I signed Matt's name. How did you know?"

"Little things." No need to confess how totally confused I'd been until I overheard them talking. The final answer hadn't fallen in place until moments ago when I realized the elusive Tom Hayden hadn't been seen by *anyone*. Then, I saw the man up close and my brain refused to slot him as Matt Crocker. "All the grants and loans Natalie got, yet your profits were minimal. Why would Bruce, who wanted the business more than anything, exit? He felt guilty for going forward after Matt's death."

Natalie's expression tightened. She thrust her shoulders forward. "He thought we should quit then and there. When the buyout offer came, he said he couldn't do it anymore. He was so determined to leave! He could have stayed with the company."

Her absolute confusion for Bruce's choices rang in her irate tone.

I felt an odd sympathy for her blindness. "It wasn't his company. You corrupted his and Matt's dream."

Part of me wondered if Matt had tried to withdraw from the devil's bargain he'd made. Should I mention it? Could my hunch be proved five years later?

The police lieutenant straightened his shoulders. "You'll all have to come to the station for questioning."

"For what?" Tom erupted. "This is water under the bridge. Matt was an orphan. He had no family."

I stared at him, dumbfounded at the man's entitlement. "The money in the trust would have gone to the next person in the Mason family line."

"How do you know there's anyone left?" Natalie's looked down her nose at me. "Matt didn't have any relatives."

"Matt didn't have any *close* relatives." I pointed to Warren Kitt, standing in silent shock to my left. "Why do you think he followed Matt's career? Why else would he check on an obscure business in Deadwood? Why would he get involved in bailing out a seemingly failing company?"

All eyes turned toward Warren.

Yvonne's jaw dropped open. "The trust would have come to you?"

Warren blinked away his surprise. "Me and my siblings."

"It still will." I crossed my arms over my chest. "Once the courts recover the money from your accounts. Warren and his family will have what they should have been theirs all along."

Natalie licked her lips. Her shocked expression gave way to a closed, thoughtful mask. "Fine. We didn't think through the implications. We thought we were doing what Matt wanted. We can make it right."

Hawken scoffed at her words. "Bruce is still dead."

Tom put out both hands. "That wasn't us."

Yvonne rose, shaking her head also. "He was our friend. We would never hurt him."

"Are you sure?" I asked the blonde. "Yvonne, do you remember what you said to Natalie in the hall yesterday as you walked toward Bruce's office?"

Her brow furrowed, then she shook her blonde curls.

I shifted my gaze to Natalie. "You said, "Why am I here? You were going to talk to him.""

Yvonne's face tightened. Suspicion filled her eyes.

"How do you know Natalie didn't see Bruce earlier? Entering through the back door. Asking him for a glass of wine." I eyed the tight-lipped brunette. "He told you I was coming. He was going to confess everything. You three were within days of leaving with the final payment. Add in all the grant money you stashed in hidden accounts and you'd be on easy street. But not if Bruce talked."

Natalie was already shaking her head. "I was just running late. I didn't get a chance to speak with Bruce. Besides, the whole town knows there was hemlock in the bottle and the glass. It's also well-known George saw Bruce open the wine bottle in his office that afternoon. I couldn't have poisoned him."

I laughed in her face. "Then you have less imagination than I do, because I'd have poured the hemlock in the open bottle after I dosed Bruce's glass."

"How dare you?" Tom stormed toward me with his fists clenched. When Hawken stepped between us, the other man stopped. "You mouthy, good for nothing busybody. You have no right to accuse my wife of murder."

"I do." Hawken spoke in a deadly voice. "I've called for back-up to transport all of you to the station."

"Since you're getting personal." I moved forward to stand next to Hawken, still staring at Tom. "How about getting justice for Matt, too? Because I have to wonder if he didn't change his mind about including you three in the partnership with him and his friend, Bruce."

Tom frowned. "What are you talking about?"

"Who was in the car at the time of the accident?" I stabbed my finger in his face. "It wouldn't happen to have been you and Natalie alone with Matt? Or perhaps just you?"

Tom retreated a step. "I didn't hurt Matt. I would never do that."

"Oh, my God! How could you?" Yvonne sobbed as she stared at her partners with a dawning horror. "It was the two of them. I never understood how Matt could have been that drunk. He told me he was going home, and he *had* changed his mind. He was going to keep control of the money."

Tom moved toward her. "Yvonne,nothing happened."

The woman sent him a scathing look."I loved Matt! We were going to be married!"

Natalie gripped her husband's arm. "You can't prove anything. I don't even remember where we buried the body."

"I do." Yvonne spoke in a chilling voice. "You two would have done anything to get your hands on that trust fund."

A wail of sirens punctuated her words.

And a quick check showed my crossword puzzle was complete. No empty squares.

***

When I rejoined my family, Marcus was jumping up and down clapping his hands. "That was so cool! We heard everything! Well, Mrs. C and I did. We were sharing the earphones."

The Belden-Tanner Detective Agency was currently driving down the road toward our home for the week.

"I have to go to the station and give a statement." I rested my hand on Kevin's shoulder as I spoke to our son. "Before I forget, Hawken wants a copy of the tape."

"Whoo-hoo!" Marcus danced in the middle of the backseat. "We get to visit the Deadwood police station! I have to get pictures, so I can e-mail them to all of our contacts."

Kevin, sitting at the wheel, looked over. "We were asked to leave the restaurant very early in your confrontation. Then, we were asked to leave the grounds."

I hid a smile behind my hand. Despite Rabi's straight face, I could only imagine Marcus's reaction to the revelations.

"All for the best really." Mrs. C sat placidly next to the twelve-year-old bundle of energy. "We listened in the comfort of the car. You put on a masterful show, ducks. Well done."

Marcus shook my shoulder. "Warren's going to get the trust fund money back, right? What about the Prairie Sun and Spirits accounts?"

The tangled web of money made my head spin. "I'm certain Warren and his brother and sister will be able to claim the money from the trust fund. If the partners stashed most of the grant and loan money they received, Warren said it could add up to millions of dollars. That was their plan all along."

Mrs. C clicked her tongue. "When Matt and Bruce objected, they were each killed in turn. Natalie and Tom are heartless tossers."

I relaxed into the seat as the tension from the face-off eased. "Yvonne didn't know about either murder. She started talking to Hawken on the way to the police car."

Marcus chuckled in glee. "Smart woman. The one who talks first gets the best deal. Remember that, everyone."

Rabi slid the boy a sideways gaze. "We won't get caught."

I laughed along with the others.

Kevin smiled into the rear view mirror at our son. "Yvonne will do time for fraud, but if they can find Matt's body, Natalie and Tom will go away for murder."

My son clapped me on the shoulder with more force than necessary. "Good job solving the case so soon! This clears up the rest of the week for sightseeing. I have a list of like twenty places. We'll start with Mount Rushmore, the Black Hills, and every ghost town within a hundred miles."

"Oh, my word." I closed my eyes. "If that doesn't scare the ghosts out of the saloons, nothing will."

"South Dakota, here we come!" Marcus howled in the backseat.

Click this link to read more adventures with Tracy and her adopted family in the Crossword Puzzle Cozy Mystery Series: https://www.amazon.com/dp/B098R27WX6

About the Author

Louise Foster is the author of the Crossword Puzzle Cozy Mystery series. She didn't pursue a writing career until well out of college. However, a lifelong love of reading and solving puzzles proved to be good training when the writing bug bit. While she enjoys reading many different types of books, from thrillers to fantasy to science fiction, mysteries have always intrigued her.

Working on jigsaw puzzles as well as crossword puzzles with her family has also been a constant part of her life. A habit that carries through to today.

In the Crossword Puzzle Mystery Series, her love of writing and solving puzzles came together. Hopefully, you'll love the quirky characters and their high-spirited adventures as much she enjoyed writing them.

Also by Louise Foster

One Across is Death (Prequel) – *Tracy and Kevin meet for the first time when she finds him standing over her dead co-worker with the murder weapon at his feet. Tracy isn't sure the handsome stranger is guilty, but how can she solve this puzzle?*

A Clue to Murder (Novella Prequel) – Two years after Tracy and Kevin meet, his landlords ask her to find their missing nephews. When her investigation leads to a dead body, she fears the worst for the two teens, but she must find the boys and finish her puzzle. (Both prequels are available on my website when you sign up for my newsletter: www.louisefoster.com)

An Ex in the Puzzle

Two Down in Tahoe

Adventures in Vegas

A Question of Murder

Five Clues to a Killer

Six Across is Murder

Seven Furlongs to a Felony

Eight Letters in Betrayal

Glue Guns for Christmas (Novella)

Made in United States
Cleveland, OH
07 June 2025

17544535R00052